"It's the gang!" breathed Tex, eyes riveted on Scarface and Kansas in the lead. The pair disappeared into the shadows of the bank entrance. The others followed. He swung toward the sheriff, standing cool and complacent, beside him. "Hell's due t' pop right now. Le's go!"

They were halfway down the courthouse steps when the shadowed quiet of the bank was shattered by the thunder of a forty-five. Another gun barked twice. The swinging door flew open and Scarface ducked out, a leather sack swinging from each hand. Kansas, guns gripped in both fists, pressed behind him. Then came Cherokee and Flatfoot, wheeling and shooting into the bank as they ran. As the door swung behind them, the blast of a shotgun within smashed the glass panels to a thousand fragments.

Across the road from the two lawmen, Wailing Willy leaped to the ponies' heads and tore the reins free from the rail.

Tex's right hand darted down. His swiveled holster jerked up and lanced fire.

Tangled Trail

ROY MANNING

ace books
A Division of Charter Communications Inc.
A GROSSET & DUNLAP COMPANY
360 Park Avenue South
New York, New York 10010

CHAPTER 1

The palms of "Tex" Tevis's hands were clammy as he crouched behind a downy white brittle bush beside the stage road where it wound through Coyote Cut. Although the scorching sun rays bit through his gray flannel shirt, the sweat lay cold upon his broad back.

Across the deep-rutted wagon trail he eyed Kansas, spare, grizzled and indifferent, rolling a smoke behind a mesquite clump. Bellied against a shelf of the gray rock that slanted up behind him, Flatfoot lay prone, watching the trail. Scarface, sullen as always, paced to and fro behind the boulders they had rolled out to block the road. Continually, his solitary eye slid up toward the lookout's prone form.

Irritably, Tex flicked off his Stetson and mopped the beaded moisture from the sweatband. What in hell was he rattled for, anyway, he asked himself savagely. This job was a pushover. Scarface might be a two-legged scorpion, but he had savvy. They'd box the stage as neatly as a mouse in a trap. A rock wall bounded one side of the narrow mountain road, on the other lay a five hundred foot drop to the rock-littered gully, from which the crows were calling, below. If the driver lashed his team and

1

made a break for it, he'd smash up on the boulders. There was no room to turn and, anyway, he'd never sight the trap until he rounded the bend, too late to pull back. Yep, Scarface, damn his snake's blood, had figured it neat.

But things still didn't set right in the young Texan's mind. He yanked his hat savagely over short, thick hair and cursed himself for a yellow quitter with the guts of a louse. Mebbe it was his first holdup, but there was no call to act like a city slicker with buck fever.

A hoarse shout from Flatfoot on the ledge above cut short the loose-jointed rider's cognitions. The lookout tumbled down the rock face, slipping and sliding over the eroding granite slope.

Kansas calmly crushed his cigarette, slipped his faded red bandanna up to eye level and slipped out a forty-five. Scarface dropped behind the boulders. The others adjusted their masks and sank out of sight.

"Cover your face, knothead!" The snarling voice of the one-eyed leader jerked back Tex's wandering thoughts. Hastily, he jerked up his blue bandanna, crouched lower and fingered the butt of his swiveled gun. Hell, he told himself in disgust, he was acting worse than a crazy colt.

For a while peace brooded over the cut. The plumed quail piped in the bush; jewel-green hummingbirds darted around the Texan's tensed form; a little blue-headed hawk circled swiftly overhead. Then, from beyond the turn in the trail, his strained ears caught the steady clip-clop of shod hooves on the ascending trail and the grinding rumble of iron-rimmed wheels, punctuated by the shrill yelps of the stage driver.

Sweat-streaked, the leaders rounded the curve, ran full tilt into the road block. The air was filled with the clatter of flying hooves as the team was thrown into plunging confusion, mingled with the frantic yells of the bearded driver as he fought, with lines wrapped around thick wrists, to bring under control the milling horses that threatened to plunge the lumbering vehicle into the depths below.

Beside him, feet braced against the footboard, sat a lank individual with a shotgun across his knees, lantern jaws champing on a chaw, eyes darting around uneasily from beneath his down-tilted Stetson. Through billowing dust, Tex glimpsed white blobs of faces peering from the stage windows.

Finally, the yelling, straining driver brought his team under control. The horses stood, bunched and snorting. . . . Scarface's yell cut through the crunch of restless hooves. "Hands up!"

Masked, he leaped up, six-shooter in each fist. In a flash the guard grabbed his shotgun, flung it to his shoulder. A gun roared. The guard slumped forward, the shotgun dropped from his limp hands and clattered to the ground. Slowly, like a rag doll, the lank figure slid over the footboard, head foremost, hit the tongue and lay in a heap between the wheeler's lashing hooves.

Tex saw a thin coil of blue smoke drifting from the muzzle of Kansas's iron.

The driver shook the lines off his wrists and flung his hands skyward. Gray-shirted, masked figures appeared on either side of the stage. One grabbed the heads of the restless leaders. The others, two aside, closed in. Tex found himself dogging Scarface.

"All out and no shenanigans!" yelled the bandit leader, emphasizing his order with a shot over the dust-covered vehicle.

Tex heard the Express box crash to the ground as the driver heaved it overside at Kansas's crisp command.

Reluctantly, the stage door creaked open and a short, paunchy drummer, mouth agape, stumbled down into the glare of the sun. A still-faced gambler in a linen duster followed, turned to assist a prim, tight-lipped woman, white lace collar stiff around her thin neck, shoes high-buttoned. Schoolmarm, figured Tex. He whistled softly as a younger woman followed. Slim and blond, finely chiseled features shaded by a wide-brimmed straw hat, she gazed around, cool, imperious blue eyes sparkling contempt.

Scarface holstered his guns, while Tex covered the four victims, and stepped close to the plump drummer. With practiced skill his big hands ran over the quaking man's clothes. He yanked a fat wallet out of a pants pocket, slipped a stickpin from the fat man's tie, tugged at a gold watch chain draped across his victim's unbuttoned vest. It slipped out easily.

"Whar's the watch?" growled the bandit.

The drummer gulped. "I—I lost it," he quavered.

With a crack Scarface's heavy hand slapped across the man's pudgy cheek. He staggered back against the stage, made a clumsy effort to duck as the bandit's bunched fist crashed into his face.

Yelping, he cowered before Scarface's bulky form, the blood streaming scarlet from his smashed nose, dripping from his chin and staining his shirt front. The bandit grabbed his fleshy throat and shook him like a hound worrying a cottontail.

"Come across or I'll throttle yuh!" growled Scarface.

The schoolmarm quietly fainted and collapsed like a bundle of rags in the gray dust.

Blubbering, the drummer fished a fine gold watch out of his boot top. The bandit grabbed it and flung him against the wheel.

Quietly, the gambler stripped a diamond ring off a middle finger and passed it over, together with a well-filled coin pouch.

Scarface dropped the loot into a pants pocket. His left hand stabbed forward and he dragged a squat derringer from its holster under the gambler's left arm. Then he seized the man's slender wrist and eyed telltale ring marks on the white, manicured fingers. His gun came out and he thrust the muzzle into the other's belly.

"Come through or I'll scatter yore guts!"

The hammer click as Scarface cocked the gun jangled on Tex's tensed nerves. He checked a mad impulse to drop the one-eyed bandit with his gun-butt.

With a resigned shrug, the gambler leaned inside the stage, fumbled beneath a seat cushion and dropped three scintillating solitaire rings into the bandit's cupped hand.

The schoolmarm was sitting up, sobbing silently.

Scarface swung to the slim blonde, grabbed at a necklace of tiny pearls that shimmered against the cream of her throat. She jerked back indignantly.

"Take your filthy paws off me, you border scum."
Bitter with contempt, her clear voice showed no
trace of fear.

Spitting out a curse, the bandit grabbed the girl's
shoulder. Her fingers clawed the bandanna off his
scarred face, his clenched fist drew back. . . .

"Lay off the gal, Scarface, or I'll plug yuh,
surer'n hell!" Behind him, the Texan's quiet drawl
was deadly with menace.

Mouthing oaths, the bandit spun around, to
meet Tex's dark eyes, flint-hard. The Texan's right
hand gripped the butt of the gun in his up-tilted
swiveled holster. "And shut that trap, or I'll close
it f'r keeps," he added. His voice rose in a yell. "Let
her roll, boys!"

The passengers hastily scrambled inside. Two of
the masked men rolled the obstructing boulders to
the roadside. Jouncing on its leather springs, the
heavy Concord lurched forward as the team
strained at the traces. In a flurry of dust it whirled
up the narrow road. Sprawled lifeless in the dust
lay the twisted body of the guard, his shotgun half
buried in the rubble.

Through the drifting fog of dust, the enraged
Scarface glared balefully at the hard-eyed Texan.
"You'll pay plenty f'r thet!" he choked.

"Mebbe so," replied the latter laconically, fingers brushing the walnut butt of his holstered gun.

While two bandits smashed open the Express
box, another led the ponies from the ravine where
they had been tied. The loot was quickly stowed in
saddle bags and the six riders clattered in the wake
of the stage. A quarter mile along the road, they
dropped down into a dry wash and struck deep
into the heart of the sun-baked hills.

* * *

Shadows slid across the sage and the distant mountains purpled into obscurity when the bandits' trail-worn ponies jogged into a brushy canyon, little more than a slit between sundered rock walls. Midway, the brush had been hacked away. On one side of the clearing, a rock stratum projected a dozen feet from the weathered wall, forming a rude shelter perhaps twenty yards long, beneath which a tall man could walk erect. Piled haphazardly beneath it were crumpled blankets, sacks of grub and oddments of saddlery. Outside, a big iron pot hung from a tripod above the cold ashes of a fire.

Dark blobs in the gloom of the canyon, the riders piled stiffly out of leather and threw off saddles and bridles. The ponies wandered across to a spring that trickled from the base of a rock pile. In silence, the saddle-sore men gathered dead wood and kindled the fire.

Cherokee, the cook, poured water into the mess of stew in the iron pot. Scarface brought out a jug of whiskey, filled a tin mug and gulped it down, refilled the mug, then passed the jug around.

Square jaw clamped on a smoke, dark eyes watching every move of the bandit leader, Tex lounged against the rock wall. The deep-etched lines across his forehead and tight set of lips made his lean, desert-tanned features somber, almost sardonic.

Sipping sullenly from his tin mug, Scarface bulked behind the fire, staring savagely at the silent figure. The leaping flames played upon his yellowed features, disfigured by a ragged scar etched blue from the socket of his sightless left eye to heavy jaw. His one beady eye glittered like a rattlesnake's but he said nothing.

Abruptly, the bandit leader disappeared into the gloom of the shelter. Tex drifted through the darkness toward the spring. The ponies were nosing at the scant herbage in the clearing. He slipped a hackamore on his buckskin. Hidden by the brush, he eased it silently toward the mouth of the canyon, tied it to the twisted trunk of a scrub oak. Then he wandered back to the firelight.

"Come and git it!" yelled Cherokee.

Eagerly the bandits crowded around the steaming pot. Each dipped his mug, filled his tin plate and hunkered around the fire. As they filled their bellies, bleak eyes shuttled between the morose features of Scarface and the silent figure on the opposite side of the crackling flames upon whom his sinister eye was focused.

The dirty dishes clattered into a pile. Tobacco sacks were jerked out and cornhusk smokes rolled. But no man moved from his place at the fire. An ominous silence draped the circle, broken suddenly by Scarface's snarl, "I got something t' say."

"I guessed it! We're lissenin'," replied Kansas. The wiry killer's voice was cold and flat.

"Tex, over there, jest joined up, but he's got big ideas. He horned in, back yonder. I'm runnin' this outfit and I gotta mind t' plug the interfering bastard."

"Why don't yuh?" drawled the Texan.

CHAPTER 2

The dry greasewood crackled loudly in the sudden silence around the campfire. Flickering flames illumined the Texan's taut features and Scarface's unshaven jowls. Kansas's pale eyes, cold and deadly, shuttled from one to the other. Flatfoot, bulky and awkward as a bull, with slobbering mouth and heavy, brutish features, sat agape, cigarette drooping from his loose lips. Cherokee's dark eyes smoldered in his dark, hatchet face. Wailing Willy, the remaining member of the gang, watery eyes set in a narrow, doleful countenance, drew a deep sigh and bared yellowed fangs in eager anticipation.

But Scarface had more coyote than cougar in his makeup. His bulk suddenly shook with a bellow of uneasy laughter.

"They's no call t' go on the prod, pard. I was jest funnin'."

"Yeah!"

"Yo're a greenhorn, in a manner of speakin', and it don't set well when yuh act out of turn. But there ain't no reason t' trade lead."

"Nope," thought Tex, "you ain't got the guts to face it out, you'd just as soon give it to me in the back." Aloud, he said:

"I don't hold with roughin' gals."

"And who," cut in Kansas, with a thin sneer, "give you the right t' be finicky?"

Tex's glance shifted to the weasel-faced killer. He had the Kansan pegged as the most dangerous man in the unsavory gang—nerveless, deadly cool and swift as a striking snake.

"I reckon I barged inter the wrong stall," he replied slowly. "Guess I'll pull out.

"The only way you go out of this outfit," spat Scarface, braced by the first gunman's stand, "is feet first."

Close by Tex stood the half-empty pot of stew, suspended from the three-legged tripod. With a swift side kick he knocked a supporting leg aside. The heavy pot toppled, spilling on the crackling fire. Instantly, the flames were doused by a torrent of cold stew and a hissing cloud of steam blotted out the forms of the hunkered outlaws. Kansas's gun lanced scarlet as the Texan threw himself flat. Barely had the slug droned through the air above him when Scarface's gun thundered. Crouching low, Tex plunged into the friendly darkness, zigzagging like a startled jackrabbit. In swift staccato, the searching guns blared behind him, awakening the echoes in rolling drum-fire that clashed from cliff to cliff.

The fugitive leaped through the low brush, panting and tripping, while hot lead snicked through the scrub and buzzed like angry pursuing bees through the air.

Ahead, he could hear the buckskin plunging and pawing wildly. Scarface's husky voice boomed from the rear:

Run f'r the mouth of the canyon and we got the bustard cornered!"

Tex bounded through whipping branches and jerked the macarty loose. The frightened pony pulled away, tugging at the tie rope. He reached forward to quiet his mount when a stabbing pain, like the thrust of a knife, shot down his left side. Gasping, he doubled up, fingers freezing on the macarty. A heavy, cloying numbness froze his leg and buttock. Spurred by the crash of Scarface and his cohorts in pursuit and the whine of lead, he straightened, fumbled at the wound with his left hand. It came away wet and sticky.

With a desperate effort he pulled himself across the restless buckskin's back, lay low over its neck and drove his spurs home. Unchecked by bit, the pony plunged frantically through the brush, while the semiconscious man on its back clutched its flying mane and swayed helplessly like a rag doll as he strove to keep his seat.

For an eternity, it seemed to the hard-hit Tex, they pounded through the darkness. Arms lacerated by thorns, face scratched by flailing branches, head spinning dizzily, he shot down the canyon and hit blindly for the solitudes.

The shouting and gunfire grew distant, died. There was no sound save the labored breathing of the galloping pony.

Tex halted it with soothing words and slid to the ground. His head whirled, he reeled against the animal's sweaty flank.

Propped by the pony, he yanked up his sodden shirt. His left side was a nerveless mass of flesh, wet with blood that drained steadily down to his boot. Exploring, his fingers found gaping holes front and rear, where a slug had punched through his body. Quickly he unknotted his bandanna and tore it into strips. Wadding one, he plugged the hole in front. But a fast-growing weakness leaded his fingers and dulled his brain. In vain, he fumbled for the wound in his back. Finally, dropping the blood-soaked rag in disgust, he wearily pulled himself across the buckskin's back. Heeling it, he hit into the night at a canter.

The jolting of the pony increased the flow of blood. A growing lassitude weighted the Texan's limbs. Slowly his body slumped forward over the buckskin's withers. The hand on the hackamore grew limp, and the animal dropped down to its customary steady jog-trot.

A spark of consciousness still glowed in the wounded man's brain. Dully he pondered on his fate. Out there in the chaos of canyons, gulches and riven hills that was the Bad Lands, a devil's dumping ground of desolation on the flanks of the Smoky Mountains, there were no living beings save lurking outlaws. By sunup, or before, the Scarface gang would hit leather and hunt him down. He was a lone wolf, spurned by law-abiding men and trailed by his own ruthless pack.

Consciousness fled and his bloodied body slid lower on the buckskin's nodding neck. Whinnying in protest, it jogged onward as a great white moon floated above the somber ridges and bathed the sleeping wilderness with cold radiance.

Sunlight streamed through the tall branches of a piñon and traced a mottled pattern upon the soogans covering Tex's long body when his eyes opened and he gazed around in startled perplexity. For a moment he thought he had awakened from a deep sleep. He jerked erect, and flopped back with an agonized gasp as a red-hot bar seemed to skewer his body. Gradually, recollection returned. Cautiously he raised his head and examined his surroundings. He was lying in a stand of piñon dotted across a shallow draw. Nearby a small spring trickled from beneath a moss-covered boulder and muddied the sandy earth. A sooted coffee pot stood amid the gray ashes of a small fire. Through the tree trunks he sighted a buckskin and a bony mule, both hobbled, browsing quietly.

His puzzlement grew when he discovered a bandage tight around his middle and he eyed the strange soogans, covered by a canvas tarp.

A cheery whistle, steadily drawing nearer, pulled his head up with a jerk and his brow knitted as he beheld an uncouth figure approaching through the pines.

The stranger was a big, gaunt, rawboned fellow with an unkempt, bushy beard and a wild mane of jet black hair curling to his shoulders. Wide open, a cheap cotton shirt exposed a thatch of dark hair on his barrel chest. Shabby pants were secured by a strip of rawhide and the bottoms thrust into scuffed high boots. A heavy gunbelt sagged around his waist and, strangest of all, he wore an ill-fitting black frock coat.

With long strides he approached the recumbent form of the wondering Texan. Piercing dark eyes, twin pieces of glass set in the dark mahogany of his desert-tanned features, surveyed the wounded man.

"The Lord be praised! He hath blessed my poor efforts to succor the afflicted. How are you feeling, friend?" Deep and forceful, his voice boomed loud from his mighty chest.

"Middlin'!" replied Tex, with the parody of a grin. "Reckon I'd be dead by now ef you hadn't crossed my trail. I'm shore thankful, mister."

"The ways of the Lord are wonderful, he noteth even the fall of a sparrow," intoned the big man sonorously.

"Wal, I'm mighty obliged t' the Lord, and not forgettin' you. Them Pearly Gates was plainer than the hump on a camel." He eyed the bearded man's frock coat and gun. "Ef I ain't speakin' out of turn, are yuh gambler, puncher or prospector?"

"I am Paul the Preacher, a humble servant of the Lord, my son, carrying the glorious message of salvation to erring souls."

"You're shore in the right spot t' find 'em. I figger four such are on my trail right now."

"Fear not, the name of the Lord is a strong tower, the righteous runneth to it and is safe."

"Not from the slugs of the Scarface gang," murmured the wounded man feelingly.

"Oh, ye of little faith!" The Preacher's voice rang with rebuke. "Were you attacked by robbers and left to perish by the wayside?"

"You said it, mister," returned Tex tersely. "And they're liable to ride this way and check up on the job."

"He who trusteth in the Lord need fear no evil," responded the Preacher indifferently. "We will refresh ourselves and then seek sanctuary."

With neither the strength nor inclination to move, the fugitive lay and watched the queer character who had saved his life kindle a fire and prepare breakfast.

He propped the helpless Tex against a saddle and brought him a pannikin of hot soup. His own big frame he nourished with flapjacks and black coffee. Appetite satisfied, he produced a sack of tobacco from a pocket in the flapping tails of his rusty frock coat and expertly built a cigarette. Hunkered close by the wounded man, he expelled the blue smoke through a great arched beak of a nose.

"Reckon I'm a bigger pest than a hydrophobic skunk," ventured Tex, as the Preacher's brooding eyes met his.

"Bear ye one another's burdens and so fulfill the law of Christ," quoted Paul. "The Lord hath sent you to be succored, I shall not fail." His eyes lifted. With a roar like that of a maddened bull, he leaped to his feet. "Git out of thet cholla, you muckle-headed, cow-hocked son of Belial!"

Tex's head swiveled in alarm. The mule had crow-hopped into a mess of cacti and stood hock deep in the malignant, thousand-spined desert growth, hammer head raised, big white teeth bared in what might well have passed for a hearty horse laugh.

The tails of his frock coat flapping against his long legs, the preacher strode purposefully toward his mount, while Tex, despite his weakness, shook with inward laughter.

The Preacher yanked his mule out of the cholla, unbuckled the hobble and proceeded to cinch on the ragged saddle which had propped Tex's head. This done, he led up the buckskin, gathered up the wounded man's six feet of bone and muscle with apparent ease and set him gently on the pony.

Tying his bedroll across the mule and dumping the cooking utensils into a gunnysack, which he tied to the saddle, he forked the animal and heeled it into an unwilling trot, leading the buckskin.

"We must journey to a place of refuge, my son,"
he rumbled, "ere these scarred evildoers, of whom
you speak, assault us with fire and thunder."

Rocking in the saddle, as waves of weakness
threatened to black out his consciousness, Tex
wrapped his fingers around the buckskin's mane
and stifled complaint behind locked lips.

It was midday when the Preacher drew rein
before the moldering remains of a tiny shack built
by some long gone prospector. It was doorless and
dilapidated. Gaps yawned in the roof, but the
peeled log walls, chinked with clay, were still intact.

Set in a deep coulee between two barren spurs of
rock that snaked down from a low-lying range of
desolate hills, the shack was hidden in thickets of
chokecherry and wait-a-bit.

Paul spread his soogans on the clean-swept earth
floor, lifted the fugitive's slumping form from the
pony and carefully laid him down. He next
stripped the gear from the animals and set about
preparing a meal.

Days passed while Tex lay in the abondoned
shack, tended by the deep-voiced preacher. His
wounds healed and his virile young body regained
its strength. Often Paul would amble off on his
mule from sunup to sundown, leaving food and
drink within reach of his patient. At other times he
would hunker by the prone figure and discourse
vigorously upon the damnation ahead for sinners
and the blessedness of salvation, pausing occasion-
ally to roll another smoke. One morning, idly

watching a couple of blue jays skittering around
the jagged holes in the roof, Tex was moved to reply to the preacher's exhortations. The bullet holes
had closed and he could feel vibrant life again surg-
ing through his veins.

Paul paused in the midst of his sermonizing,
added another butt to the litter that steadily grew
on the bare earth floor and dug into his coat tails
for the makin's.

"Yo're all wool and a yard wide, Preacher,"
drawled Tex, "but I ain't subscribing to yore ideas.
No siree! Take them dog-blasted sinners, now.
They may git fire and brimstone aplenty in the next
world, but they sure cash in before they shuffle off.
My notion is, grab when the grabbin's good and
take a chance of runnin' past St. Peter."

"Woe is me!" bellowed Paul, spilling his half-
made cigarette in the shock of righteous indignation. "Oh, thrice ungrateful sinner! The Lord,
through me, his humble servant, yanked yuh
plumb out of the shadow of death and now you
turn your back upon him! Alas, that the seed
should have fallen upon such barren ground." He
balled the makin's, ran his tongue across the paper
and eyed Tex reproachfully.

"I used t' hit the straight and narrow trail," persisted the Texan obstinately, "but it don't pay. No
siree!"

"Better poverty for a brief spell than hellfire for
Eternity," boomed Paul.

"I ain't objectin' t' poverty, but t' all-fired human cussedness."

"Unburden your soul, my misguided young
friend, and we will wrestle with the devil together."

The Preacher touched a match to the tube of tobacco. His piercing blue eyes dwelt on the invalid expectantly.

"Wal, Tom, that's my brother, and me brought a herd up the Chisholm Trail. We found a buyer at Dodge City and hit west, our money-belts stuffed with gold, figgerin' we'd homestead a likely spot and run a small herd. Wal, we located in Smoky Valley, filed our claims in the land office at Hanging Wells and run our stuff in the foothills. We built a right dandy ranch house and barn, too, and sure shrunk them money-belts. Everything was hunky-dory." Then his quiet, even voice hardened. "Colonel Cresswell figgers he's cattle king of Concha County. Lays claim t' the hull length and breadth of Smoky Valley—two hundred square miles—but I bet he never paid a dollar or got a document t' show f'r it. Cows carries his Box-C iron from Twin Buttes t' the border. I gamble he rode a dozen ranches. Wal, his punchers serve notice on us t' git out. We stick—it's our land. They haze our stock, fence off the wells, then smoke us out. When they put the torch t' the spread, they cut down Tom. I make a break, ride f'r the county seat. The lawmen give me the haw-haw, sez textbook law don't go in Arizona, and git t' hell for a dog-goned measly nester. So I hit the lobo trail and throw in with Scarface. You wanna take the gospel to Hanging Wells," he concluded, his voice harsh with bitterness.

"A fool in his folly!" roared Paul. "A poor weakling, tested by the good Lord, tried in the fires of adversity—and found wanting!" He paced the shack with mighty strides, glaring at Tex's bleak countenance. "Whar's your guts? Are you a yellow quitter, that you allow an upstart, a prince of darkness, to hound you to the hangman? Kin yuh use a gun?" He paused, gazed accusingly at the tight-lipped Texan.

"Faster'n most."

"Then fight these minions of evil, fight them righteously and lawfully. The evil bow before the good and the wicked at the gates of the righteous."

"That sounds strange from a preacher," growled Tex argumentatively. "Ain't I heard of returnin' good f'r evil?"

"Quote not the Good Book against me," roared Paul. "The Lord chooseth his own weapons. Git a splint for thet backbone and overthrow the powers of darkness. Have I grabbed you at the gates of death, nurtured you these many days, to see your eternal soul descend into the scorching fires of perdition? Turn from the crooked trail, my brother! Rise up and smite the oppressor, but lawfully—yea, lawfully!"

"You're a mighty powerful argyfier," mused Tex.

"My strength is the Lord's, none shall overcome it. Now git busy and practice thet draw!" With this exhortation, the Preacher strode wrathfully from the shack.

The young Texan pondered long upon the unorthodox preacher's observations. Slowly, resolve crystallized in his brain. He would return to Hanging Wells, to repay the debt he owed this burly desert evangelist. He would admit conversion and swear to stick to the straight and narrow path. But he would go back as an avenger, to seek out and ruthlessly destroy the leader of the punchers who had murdered his brother and destroyed their home.

So, one dawn found him, strength regained, gun-hand supple, hitting through the hills, while the rising sun gilded the barrens with glistening gold and touched the ragged peaks of the distant Chiracuhuas with crimson—as though they had been dipped in blood.

CHAPTER 3

The sun was high when a lean dust-powdered rider
on a sweat-streaked buckskin jogged past the dirty
white adobes that fringed the county seat. Hanging
Wells was a replica of a dozen other cow towns set
on the fringe of the burning desert or squatting
amid the foothills. False-fronted stores and saloons
bounded a wide street, pocked by iron-shod hooves
and rutted deep by wagons. Above the huddle of
wooden structures in the center of town rose the
big, box-like county courthouse, approached by a
wide flight of wooden steps. Set opposite, kitty-
corner, were the faded awnings of the two-story
Travelers Hotel and the Concha County Bank.
Staining the sky above the foothills far beyond the
valley, the smelters of the Concha Copper Company belched lazy trailers of twisting smoke.

As the buckskin's hooves stirred the dust, Tex's
eyes swept the shadowed sidewalks; for this was the
stamping ground of the man he had sworn to kill.
Few were abroad at the siesta hour—indolent Mexicans dozed in shady alleys, or lounged against
store fronts, swarthy features hidden by widespread sombreros. A scattering of ponies drooped
at the chain of hitch rails. From a huge cask,
hauled by a team of skinny burros, an ancient
zanzero, or water carrier, refilled upended barrels

set like sentinels along the plankwalks.

Ahead, thrusting out of the level street like an islet in a placid ocean, the rider's eyes dwelt reflectively on Hanging Wells' pride and joy—the Hangman's Oak. Legend said that a dozen of Black Barney's Cutthroats had been hung up to dry by irate citizens from the gnarled limbs of the mighty tree, following an attempted jail delivery. Hallowed by tradition, the landmark was ringed by a circle of whitewashed boulders, with a convenient bench where old-timers sought the shade. Some said that the choking death gurgles of the long-dead bandits could be heard in the still, small hours, but these yarns usually emanated from highly liquored gents ejected from the saloons around midnight.

At random, Tex kneed his pony to the hitch rail in front of a saloon that sported a tarnished painting of a huge coin and the legend "The Double Eagle" over the peeling paint of its batwings.

Knotting his reins around the smooth-worn rail, he ducked beneath it and pushed through to the sawdust-covered floor. For a few moments his vision was blurred by the transition from glaring sunlight to the dimness of the long, low-ceilinged saloon. Then he glimpsed an array of deserted card tables, a long plank bar, and—he blinked—a girl nonchalantly polishing glasses behind the bar.

The Texan's lips curled in quick disgust. When a man craved the company of jades he sought a dancehall, when he craved a drink he wanted to be served by a man, not a brazen, painted hussy. In indecision, he checked his eager pace and half-turned toward the street, but he was already halfway across the saloon.

With reluctant steps he advanced to the liquor-stained bar . . . and quickly reversed his snap judgment.

This was no scented, smirking hussy. The lithe young white-aproned girl was crowned by a thick coil of glinting, coppery hair spiraled around her small head. There was none of the flawless beauty of the cool blonde aboard the stage in her snub nose and freckled features, but her eyes glowed with animation, her lips were firm and red and she moved with easy grace.

Fire sparkled in her dark eyes as she watched the tall rider. He guessed she had noted his impulse to retreat.

"Well, mister?" There was a challenge in her throaty voice.

He crooked his elbows on the bar, leaned forward and regarded her quizzically. "A gal like you don't belong behind a bar," he drawled.

"When I want your opinion, stranger, I'll ask for it," she snapped. "Name your pison or get out!"

Tex grinned. "Slug o' bourbon, sister. How come you tendin' bar?"

"My paw, Pat O'Keefe, runs this saloon, if it's any of your business." The fiery little redhead slammed a bottle before him and slid a glass up beside it.

"Nice gals don't hang around saloons," he commented severely. Pouring two fingers, he gratefully washed the trail dust out of his throat and again tilted the bottle.

"Drunken saddle-stiffs who waste their wages in saloons wouldn't know a nice girl if they met one," she retorted with cutting emphasis, and turned her back on him. He caught her stormy eyes in the long mirror back of the bar.

"Say, you look prettier than a painted wagon when you're angry," he chuckled. Then his jaw clamped with a click as he sighted a tall, spare individual, star glittering on his loose-hanging vest, quietly easing up from the rear.

The newcomer's features were long and bony, his skin dried out and wrinkled like musty parchment. A sparse, sandy mustache straggled from beneath his long thin nose.

Inwardly tensed, Tex tossed off his second drink and fumbled for the makin's.

"Reckon you better come along with me," grated a dry voice at his elbow.

He straightened and swung around, to face heavy-lidded eyes, colorless and unblinking.

Sheriff Dan Cummings's thumbs were hooked in his sagging gun-belt and Tex's swift, appraising gaze noted a bony right hand was mighty close to the curved butt of his holstered gun.

"What's the big idea?" demanded the Texan. "I just rode inter town."

"Yuh wouldn't have been ridin' with Scarface?" Quick panic gripped Tex, impulsively his right hand flashed down toward his holster, but the cool-eyed lawman was quicker. His .45 flicked up and out, the black muzzle nudged Tex's sore ribs.

"Stick 'em up," grated the sheriff, "or they'll tote yuh t' Dock Hoskins's undertakin' parlor."

Hands shoulder high, Tex backed against the bar. The sheriff grabbed his gun with practiced ease and thrust it beneath his waistband.

Inwardly, the Texan surged with conflicting emotions. Anger that he had followed the

Preacher's advice and headed for Hanging Wells, amazement that his brief tie-up with the Scarface gang should be so widely known, rage that he had allowed himself to be taken prisoner so tamely.

"How come yuh put the finger on me?" he growled.

"The birdies chirp when I'm around," returned the lawman cryptically. "Le's git going!"

Side by side, they threaded between the empty tables, stepped outside and thudded along the hollow plankwalk toward the courthouse, bulking high along the quiet street.

A rider and a girl in a bright red shirtwaist stepped out of the hotel and crossed the street. Tex's eyes followed the patch of brilliant color against the gray dust, then widened as the pair drew close. There was no mistaking the slim figure, pale perfection of features and sun-flecked blond hair—it was the girl of the stage. He sent up a silent prayer of thankfulness that he had been masked.

"Howdy, Dan!" At the sound of her companion's deep voice as he greeted the sheriff, the prisoner's eyes swiveled toward him, and hardened into twin points of bleak rage. Again he stabbed for his gun. He mouthed a bitter curse as his hand dropped away from the empty holster.

With the quick grace of a panther the girl's escort dropped into a crouch at the threatening motion. Ready right hand slapped his gun-butt. As quickly, he noted Tex's empty holster and straightened with a mocking grin.

He was a lean, muscular fellow, arrayed in stylish pearl-gray Stetson, silk shirt and heavy goatskin chaps. His gun-belt sparkled with silver conchas. A heavy gold watch chain spanned his middle. His features were copper-colored, with heavy, jutting jaw. Hard, reckless eyes taunted the tensed Texan from above high cheekbones.

"So you're the Texas nester from Indian Bluff!" His teeth flashed. "Wal, we got yore pard, figgered we plugged you. Better ride wide of Box-C range, mister!"

"I ain't sidesteppin' you or yore murderin' Box-C polecats."

"Wal, stick around ef yuh crave t' swap lead," returned the dark-featured rider carelessly, "—after you're done plaitin' hair bridles."

At the sound of Tex's voice a startled light leaped into the girl's eyes. Her mouth opened, then quickly clamped shut.

The pair moved on.

"Who was that hombre?" demanded Tex of the spare figure at his side.

"Monte Moreland, foreman of the Box-C," replied the sheriff. "Looked like you was acquainted," he added dryly.

"Thet measly sidewinder rodded the gang thet put the torch t' my spread."

"They scotch nesters quickern' rattlesnakes in Smoky Valley."

"Nesters, hell!" burst out the angry Texan. "We filed on thet land."

"Mebbeso!" returned the sheriff incuriously.

Lodged in an eight-by-ten cell in the basement of the courthouse, Tex hunched on the straw mattress of his narrow bunk and gloomily considered the swift smash of his hopes and plans. With furrowed brow he reviewed the misfortunes that had dogged him since he and his brother had headed west with fat money-belts and high hopes. Tom killed, money gone, cows rustled, buildings burned. His lapse into crime and now the bitter retribution. A black-paged past and a future bounded by the granite walls of Tucson penitentiary.

Feverishly he jumped up, paced the narrow cell. Before he was buried in the living tomb of Tucson, he'd get that grinning half-Indian, Box-C foreman Moreland—the wolf who had brought disaster upon him. By the faint light that filtered through a barred grating high above his head he eagerly examined his cage. Three sides were bounded by steel bars; the fourth, apparently the side of the building, by stout planks spiked to great baulks of timber. The grating, through which a slim finger of sunlight stabbed through the obscurity and patched the dirt fioor, was out of reach. Even if the bars were removed, it would scarcely admit his head.

Imperceptibly, the patch of sunlight inched across the floor and climbed the dull bars as the hours dragged by. Keys rattled. The sheriff pushed a lurching drunk into the cell opposite and lit an oil lamp bracketed at the end of the passageway.

Tex huddled on his bunk, the drunk's snoring heavy in his ears. "What the hell," he thought morosely, "does the Preacher know about life? He's never been smoked out, hunted, robbed. Reckon he wouldn't run off at the mouth so danged freely if he was a homeless cur with every man's boot in his ribs, and no one on his side.

The sun had gone now. The only illumination came from the sickly yellow rays of the oil lamp, feebly beating back the shadows.

A sharp rap on the grating above brought the

dispirited Texan's head up in quick curiosity. Something white was pushed between the bars and fluttered down, to rest almost at his feet. He reached forward and picked up a folded sheet of white paper. Spreading it upon his knee, he read: "You were riding from Coyote Creek to Squall Ridge before you quit and rode into town." That was all. No signature, no explanation of the strange message.

With a frown of perplexity he reread the words, written in a slanting feminine hand.

"What the heck's it all about?" he muttered. Quickly he crumpled the sheet and thrust it into a pants pocket as a deputy pushed open the heavy outside door and entered with the prisoners' supper on a tray.

Still pondering, Tex grabbed the pot of coffee and plate of beans that were pushed through the trap in his cell door.

CHAPTER 4

From long habit, Tex was astir when pale fingers of dawn probed through the grating. Like a caged animal, he restlessly roamed the cell, pondering on the message that had fluttered to his feet. Who had sent it? There was only one answer—the girl on the stage. Her blue eyes had telegraphed recognition when he challenged Monte Moreland, the Box-C foreman, and he had seen small teeth bite down upon her lower lip as she hastily checked a spontaneous greeting. Some women fuss and faint under stress, some are stimulated. The cool blonde was one of the latter. She was a thoroughbred, just the type to help a fellow in a jam. But what in heck did she mean by riding from Coyote Creek to Squall Ridge?

A burly deputy had clumped away with the breakfast dishes and booted out the woozy-eyed, chastened drunk, when the outside door creaked open and Sheriff Cummings stepped into the passageway that ran midway between the cells, jangling a ring of keys. Bald, sunbrowned dome polished like a lava knob, eyes heavy-lidded, he reminded the prisoner of an old bald eagle—unwinking and alert.

Behind him strode a tall, squarely built cowman, gray flannel shirt wrinkled and crumbled with tobacco, earth-stained pants stuffed into high boots. But his face attracted the Texan's eyes. The desert-eroded features were as cold and expressionless as weathered granite. Only his eyes were alive; restless and piercing. A jutting jaw clamped his mouth as tight as a rat-trap. Sweat-streaked, an old Stetson was jammed down upon a mat of light brown hair. The swing of his broad shoulders and the cold arrogance smoldering in his eyes proclaimed that here was a man accustomed to leadership, a man who had battled ahead by sheer dominance of will, a man of resistless energy. An overbearing tyrant, and certainly a tough hombre to cross.

"Wal, here he is!" snapped Cummings, jerking his head toward Tex who, unshaven and tousle-headed, lounged against the bars.

Flinty-blue eyes bored into the prisoner like gimlets.

"Sure, that's Tex!" rapped out the visitor in harsh, vibrant tones. "Been with me since spring round-up. Quit two days back. What did yuh lock him up f'r—drunk, as usual?"

"Nope!" The wondering Texan saw perplexity mirrored in the sheriff's deep-sunk eyes. "Gotta tip he was trailing with Scarface." He addressed the prisoner. "What kinda chores did yuh handle round the Colonel's spread—toppin' broncs?"

"Rode line from Coyote Creek to Squall Ridge," returned Tex laconically.

"Reckon that cinches it," acknowledged Cummings. "I'll rawhide thet blasted hand f'r runnin' out on me."

The cowman snorted, swung briskly on his heel and jingled down the passageway. The sheriff selected a key from the bunch that dangled from the huge ring, clicked back the lock and eased the barred door open.

No longer wondering, Tex stepped out. It was plain that the tough, sorrel-topped cowman was the blonde's father. He did not doubt that her quick mind had devised the trick that had secured his release. A gal like that, he thought, was the kind a fellow could tie to.

He followed the sherrif along a dim passageway and up a flight of wooden stairs, emerging in a broad corridor that ran the depth of the courthouse. The sheriff's office was in front, over-looking the street. Without comment, Cummings slid open a drawer in his flat-top desk, picked Tex's iron from a dozen tagged guns and extended it to the waiting rider.

The Texan pressed the release key under the gun, removed the cylinder with one hand and shook the cartridges out. Replacing it, he slid the pin home. Then he reloaded and lowered the hammer gently on an empty chamber.

Cummings watched the procedure in silence. "Takin' no chances, eh?" he commented acidly, as Tex holstered the gun.

"Why should I?" drawled Tex. "And next time, mister, don't be in such an all-fired hurry t' clap law-abidin' citizens in the cooler."

The sheriff's thin features twisted in disgust. "They's only one reason you ain't there right now, wise guy—ain't nobody in Concha County durst call the Colonel a doggone liár." He hooked his swivel chair irritably with his foot, jerked it back and jackknifed into it. Thoughtfully, Tex moved toward the corridor. As he pushed through the heavy door that fronted the courthouse and stepped into the sunshine, the Colonel was swinging across the broad back of a handsome black.

"Hey!" bawled Tex, and took the wide stairway at a run to voice his thanks. But without a backward glance, set stiff and upright in the high pommeled saddle, the poker-faced cowman drove home the steel and drummed down the street.

Tex grabbed the arm of a puncher who sauntered by. "Say, bud, who's thet man? He nodded toward the rapidly disappearing rider, veiled in rising dust fog.

"Colonel Cresswell, rods the Box-C. Thought every man in Concha County was acquainted with the old rannakin." For a moment Tex stood stock still, as the significance of the carelessly spoken words sank home. The puncher eyed his set features queerly and strolled on. "Colonel Cresswell!" muttered Tex thickly. "Thet's the bustard whose crew kilt Tom and put the torch to our spread."

An hour later, shaved, and hair still damp from a bath in the back room of the barber's shack, the Texan sat at a table beside the fly-specked window of The Last Chance. Taking occasional draughts from a bottle of beer, he watched the velvet-trousered Mexicans and bow-legged riders drift by and cogitated upon his future course. One point was clear, the blood of his brother cried for Monte Moreland's life and he was determined to match cutters with the reckless-eyed Box-C foreman. But Colonel Cresswell was the king-pin. He was the tyrant who rodded Smoky Valley, bossed the lawmen and treated decent settlers like hoboes.

Until Cresswell's hold was broken no small cowman could get a toe hold in the valley or in the far-flung foothills that lay beyond. The law meant nothing to the granite-faced Colonel—he was the law—and the young Texan's gorge rose at the thought.

Brain busy, dead cigarette drooping from his lips, Tex gazed out upon the sun-swept street. Suddenly, his attention quickened. A bony mule ambled slowly along the wagon ruts. Perched on its back, long legs dangling, was a frock-coated figure with a disordered mane of black hair and bushy beard. One hand held the reins, the other clutched a bulky book.

"The Preacher!" ejaculated Tex. He jumped to his feet and hastened through the batwings. At his hail, the Preacher jerked the animal to a willing stop. His roar of greeting scared a questing cur into yelping retreat.

"Ah, the prodigal!" He stepped off the mule, big paw crushing the Texan's outstretched hand.

"Fresh outa the hoosegow," grinned Tex.

"Bring my soul out of prison, that I shall praise thy name," intoned the Preacher. "Harsh is the way of the transgressor."

"But I ain't a transgressor," remonstrated Tex wryly. "Somebody turned me in f'r ridin' with Scarface."

"And the Lord accomplished thy liberation," added the Preacher triumphantly.

"The devil!" exploded Tex. "It was thet Cresswell bustard, the hairpin who rods the Valley. I'd 'a' sooner hung."

"You speak in parables, my son," boomed Paul.

"Let us seek shelter from the heat of the day."

Bulky Bible cuddled against his rusty coat, he led the mule to the nearest hitch rail and—followed by the astonished Tex—strode without hesitation into the Double Eagle.

"Greetings, my prairie flower!" he roared to the sparkling-eyed Kathryn O'Keefe, behind the bar. "I crave a glass of God's nectar, nature's undiluted beverage." Dimpling, she poured a glass of water and pushed it toward him. Her smile faded as she turned primly to the Texan.

"Make mine a bourbon; my innards rust ef I drink water," he said gravely, tossing two dollars on the bar. "Reckon I owe f'r the last two drinks."

With unsmiling features the girl pushed over bottle and glass. A fifty-cent piece clinked beside him, as he poured a short drink. With a slow grin that showed even white teeth and changed the whole complexion of his sober countenance, he pushed the coin back. "Thet's for the smile, ma'am." He chuckled at her indignant gasp as he moved toward the table where the Preacher had deposited his Bible and taken a seat.

Paul dabbed the moisture off his damp brow and sipped the lukewarm water with zest. Tex gulped his drink and eyed the Preacher humorously. "Didn't figger you'd set foot in one of these here sinks of iniquity."

"I would carry the Lord's message to the depths of hell," declared Paul, with flashing eyes. "Where else is the Word more needed than such spots as this, where sinners poison the bodies a bountiful Creator gave them with strong drink and choke their lungs with the smoke of a filthy weed." As he spoke he dexterously rolled a quirley. Tex caught a gleam of humor in his deep eyes.

"You got me roped and tied with them argyments," acknowledged the Texan, with a smile. He dropped his jocular tones. "I ain't no great shakes as a glory boy, Preacher. Looks like I done tangled my rope already." He told of his arrest and release through the good offices of Colonel Cresswell's daughter. "I done decided," he concluded, "t' hang up Monte Moreland's hide, and hightail."

"Alas," groaned the Preacher, "that the seed I sowed with such loving kindness fell upon stony ground. The Lord is at your right hand, my son, he will deliver you from your enemies, though they be as locusts. I am sorely disappointed. Have I brought you back from the gates of death to be a cheap gunfighter? Are you blind to the glorious privilege of bringing low this Goliath who holds the Valley under his thrall?"

"But my chances of bustin' Colonel Cresswell ain't worth a hoot in hell," expostulated Tex.

"To the Lord everything is possible," returned the Preacher serenely. "Did he not make the blind to see and the lame to walk?" His voice rose in deep fervency, he pounded the table with his mighty fist until the glasses rattled. "Stick around, oh ye of little faith! Flee not from thine adversary. If ye have faith as a grain of mustard seed, ye shall say unto this mountain, remove hence to yonder place and it shall remove, and nothing shall be impossible to you. The Lord will show the way to overcome this spawn of the devil, but lawfully, yea lawfully."

"I'll stick around, ef you say so," agreed Tex grudgingly. "But you tell the Lord t' keep Moreland outa Hanging Wells, or one of us is plumb liable to go to hell."

"And I saw in you a flaming sword, to drive iniquity out of Smoky Valley," sighed the Preacher.
He rose, gathered up his book. "The Lord's ways
are devious, my son, you may yet be his appointed
instrument. Adios!" Black beard outthrust, he
bellowed farewell to Kathryn O'Keefe and strode
majestically toward the batwings.

At a loose end, Tex ate his midday meal in the
steamy Chinese restaurant, rolled a cigarette and
wandered along the plankwalk, eyes alert for the
Box-C foreman's dandified figure. Sheriff
Cummings's spare form appeared at the door of a
saloon. At sight of Tex he approached briskly.
"Been huntin' you," he grunted. "Come on up t'
the office."

Eyes guarded, the Texan froze in his tracks,
watching Cummings's gun hand. A pony switched
its tail at the rail close by. Before he'd go into a cell
again, Tex decided swiftly, he'd wing the lawman and make a break for it—Preacher or no
preacher.

"What's the charge?" His voice was brittle.

"This ain't no arrest—it's jest a friendly powwow." Cummings's leathery features twisted in a
grin. Like a buzzard, thought Tex.

Stiff-legged, like a wary terrier alert for trouble, he
swung beside the sheriff and paced him to the
courthouse.

Cummings scaled his hat toward a peg, slid open
a drawer of his desk and pulled out a box of cigars.

"Help yourself!" he invited, setting the box on
the desk top. He selected a smoke himself and bit
off the end with yellowed teeth.

Cautiously Tex lifted out a bone-dry stogie, sat

down gingerly in a straight-back chair and touched a match to the cigar. "Reckon the old coot figgers I'll tip off the gang's hideout," he thought. "Wal, I ain't thet yeller."

Cummings sank down in the swivel chair, stretched out his long legs and fixed the Texan with his colorless stare.

"Could yuh use five thousand dollars?" he queried abruptly.

"Not f'r a double-cross."

"Double-cross—who?" Cummings's voice was dry.

The Texan shrugged. "I'm jest stating general principles."

"Wal, this ain't no double-cross. I want a fast gun hand, with guts and savvy, and I pegged you f'r the job. Ever hear of the Concha Copper Company?" He motioned toward the black smoke that hung over the distant hills.

"Ain't they runnin' a smelter, 'way west?"

"Yep, and they git a big payroll on the first of each month—in gold—if some fast-shootin' gents don't knock it off. The company sends a spring wagon in f'r the gold, with two mounted guards. The county pervides a deputy with a shotgun. Last two trips the deputies was shot as full of holes as a salt-shaker—and the payroll vamoosed. They's a five thousand dollar reward for recovery of the gold or capture of the hell-raisers. How does it sound?"

"Yuh figger I'm locoed enough t' tote the shotgun and take a quick trip t' Kingdom Come?" Tex's voice was derisive.

"Guess again! I want yuh t' hit the trail of them payroll snatchers. It calls f'r guts," he added, as an afterthought.

Tex sucked the cigar and met the sheriff's cold
stare.

"I'll take yuh!" he said suddenly.

Cummings's wrinkled features crinkled in what
passed for a smile. He fumbled in the desk and
tossed a deputy sheriff's badge to the loose-limbed
figure, now relaxed in the straight-back chair.
"Hold up yuhr right hand and repeat after me." He
mumbled rapidly and concluded with a brisk "yuhr
deputized!"

Tex's brain worked rapidly as he pinned the
badge inside his shirt. Yesterday a prisoner, facing
a term in the penitentiary; today a deputy, backed
by the authority of the law. What was that the
Preacher said? His head snapped up.

"Has thet Preacher Paul gotta hand in this?"

The sheriff stared blankly. "Say, this ain't no
prayer meeting."

Shadows edged across the street as Tex thumped
down the courthouse steps. Two riders pounded
past with shrill yippees. Dust swirled and eddied as
others clip-clopped over the sun-baked ground.
Ponies milled and kicked at the hitch rails as six-
guns roared from a bunch of yelling punchers. A
piano tinkled off key in a nearby saloon. He
paused, puzzled by the excitement, then his lips
twisted with an understanding smile—it was the
last day of the month, payday.

He drifted along the plankwalk, jostled by yam-
mering punchers. Abruptly he jerked to a stop. The
light of a swinging oil lamp shone directly on the
dark features of a bulky rider pushing into a
saloon. There was no mistaking the deep blue scar
etched from eye to mouth—it was Scarface.

CHAPTER 5

"Wal, ef it ain't the ladies' man!" A thin rasping voice at his elbow brought Tex's head around as Scarface shouldered into the crowded saloon.

He looked down into the wizened features of Kansas, the acid-faced gunman's talon-like fingers crooked above the holster thonged to his right leg, his tight slit of a mouth twisted sideways in a snarl as he met the tall Texan's eyes. A hard shoulder butted Tex from behind as his muscles set for a quick draw. Swung around by the impact, he discovered Cherokee's dark features. Around the trio, bunched in the gloom of the canopied plankwalk, flowed a stream of smoking, swearing punchers and vaqueros, spilling from the saloons, ducking under the hitch rails, hailing each other with friendly invective.

With Cherokee at his back and Kansas fronting him, both fast implacable gunmen, a cold premonition of death prickled the young Texan's spine. Either would kill as casually as they would touch a match to a cigarette. If he beat Kansas to the draw, the half-breed would drill him.

He thought fast, forced a grin. "You boys hit town f'r a little celebratin'?"

"You'd be surprised!" growled Kansas. Still restlessly clawing his gun, he hesitated, for once seemed at a loss. "Le's have a drink!" he finally blurted.

As much a prisoner as though he were manacled, the Texan jingled over the creaking planks between the two bandits. Close-herded, he pushed into The Last Chance. Smoke-veiled, the brass lamps suspended from the rafters bathed the packed saloon with yellow light. His eyes ran over the scattered card tables, clustered with sweating punchers, seeking Scarface. Flannel-shirted men stood thick at the bar, yelling for drinks at overworked barkeeps. Through the drone of voices, tinkle of glasses and clink of poker chips, a tinny melody jingled from a scarred piano, set against a side wall.

Kansas shouldered the Texan toward a table in a far corner. Around it were hunched Flatfoot's bulky body, the doleful Wailing Willy and the scarred leader's form. On the table were set two bottles of whiskey, rapidly emptying.

"Look what we stubbed our toe on, Chief!" snarled Kansas, as the trio elbowed close through the boisterous throng.

Scarface twisted his head to see with his one good eye, half-filled glass in hand. He focused Tex's tight stare, choked on the liquor and spat out a curse. His chair overturned with a bang, as he dabbed spasmodically for his gun and leaped to his feet.

"Don't upset the wagon!" spat Kansas, grabbing the scarred man's bent arm. He righted the chair, pushed the fuming Scarface into it, bent over and whispered into his ear. Impelled by the nudge of Cherokee's gun in the small of his back, Tex seated himself and met the baleful stare of the bandits. As they watched, he slipped his right hand beneath his unbuttoned shirt, unpinned the deputy's badge and carelessly stuck it on his loose-hanging vest.

A thunderbolt could not have produced a more devastating effect. Flatface's heavy jaw dropped limply. Willy's red-rimmed eyes protruded in a fascinated stare. Scarface's puckered scar burned black against his whitening features. Only the Kansan was unmoved. He fixed the glittering star with a venomous stare.

Tex tilted a whiskey bottle and poured himself a drink. "Reckon you boys better hit leather," he suggested casually.

"You dirty double-crosser!" choked Scarface. Again his fingers closed upon the black butt of the gun sagging from his hip. "You need pisonin'— lead pisonin'." In a flash Kansas's sinewy fingers fastened on his gun arm. "Git a holt on yoreself!" he rasped. His bleak eyes sought the nonchalant Tex. "Figger you got us jiggerrood, smart guy? Jest one slug ull stop yore clock."

"And swing the Scarface gang!" Tex's voice was brittle. Outwardly composed, his stomach knotted as he awaited the impact of a bullet from Cherokee, hovering like a black shadow behind his chair. Relief flooded his tensed form as he glimpsed the star of burly Plug Hawkins, the jailor, close by in the throng. Scarface's quick eye swiveled and followed the direction of his intense glance.

"No need t' git ringy!" The bandit chief's heavy lips pulled back from yellowed fangs in a grisly smile. He leaned forward. "Le's call it quits, Tex! Let bygones be bygones. We jest rode in t' flap our wings and crow. Heah, have another drink!"

He slopped whiskey into the Texan's glass, and refilled his own. "You ride yore trail and we'll ride ours.

"Did I bust in on you?" demanded Tex.

"You shore didn't," agreed Scarface placatingly.

"Then whyfore are yuh belly-achin'? Adios, amigos!" His voice was mocking as he rose. Death in his gleaming eyes, Kansas listened, thin lips locked. Around the tensed group, the rumble of many voices reverberated against the low ceiling, the plaintive notes of the piano breaking through whenever the surge of sound momentarily subsided.

Knifing through the crowd, Tex gained the street. With a gasp of heartfelt relief he inhaled lungfuls of the cool night air and dabbed his damp brow. After a quick glance over his shoulder to check if the gang was keeping cases on him, he slipped into a dark alley that ran between the saloon and the barber's next door, stumbled over an empty crate, sank down upon it to collect his scrambled thoughts.

Why had the gang allowed him to leave that saloon alive? There was only one answer—they dared not start a fracas and draw attention to their presence in Hanging Wells. Something big was afoot, beside which his killing was incidental. What was big enough to compel these wolves to stifle their hatred and allow him to walk out unscathed? In a blinding flash light broke upon him—the Concha Copper Company's payroll. That was the magnet which had drawn them to the county seat.

He rose, stepped toward the plankwalk, then pulled back into the gloom of the alley. Maybe they would chance a bullet or a knife in the crowded street. Fumbling down the inky alleyway, he emerged at the rear of the saloon. The lamplight that flooded from the back windows revealed a deserted stretch of waste ground, littered with bottles and empty cans, extending the length of the block. Stumbling over piles of rubbish and threading between garbage tubs, Tex streaked for the courthouse.

Sucking the stem of a corncob pipe, and owlish behind a pair of steel-rimmed spectacles, Sheriff Cummings was shuffling through papers on his desk. Self-consciously, he snapped off the glasses and slipped them beneath the papers when Tex burst into the office.

"When does the Concha Copper payroll go out?" demanded Tex breathlessly.

"Tomorrow," snapped Cummings. "What's eatin' yuh?"

"The Scarface gang's in town."

"How many?"

"Five."

The gritty wheels of his chair squeaked as the sheriff thrust it back and stretched for his gun-belt. "Stick around. I'll go get a posse and jug the galoots."

"On whose say-so?"

Cummings buckled his belt. "Yores, who else?" he growled irritably.

"Nope!" returned Tex brusquely. "I'm no squealer."

"So yuh ran with the gang?" The sheriff's voice was sharp-edged. "I got the deadwood on yuh now. You jug them or I jug you."

Tex met his bleak stare. "Go ahead!" he taunted. "Stick me in the cooler while the gang pry that payroll loose! Use yuhr head, Sheriff. Set down!"

Dan Cummings had not rodded the law for twenty years without adding a big slice of diplomacy to a healthy stock of common sense. He read determination in the Texan's steady eyes and set of his lean jaw.

With a grunt, he sank back into his seat, pulled out his discolored corncob and stuffed the bowl. "What's on yuhr mind?" he inquired mildly.

"How d'ye handle the payroll?"

"Express company unloads it off the five-thirty mixed freight tomorrow morning. Jem Barlow, the agent, wheels it up t' the bank in a hand truck, with four armed guards. I stick around too. A spring wagon from the smelter picks it up at noon—three armed men on the wagon and six outriders. They're takin' no chances this trip."

"Much movin' at five-thirty?"

"Not a shadder. Nobody stirs around town much afore seven."

Tex rolled a smoke, brow furrowed. "Not much chance t' grab the dinero outside the bank. Scarface ain't got but four men," he mused. "Any guards inside?"

"Manager and two clerks. The gold's always been lifted on the trail, the getaway's easier."

"I'll gamble thet Scarface outfit busts yore bank wide open sometime afore noon," announced Tex decisively.

Cummings tugged at his faded mustache, eyeing the Texan thoughtfully. "Mebbe you're right," he finally acknowledged. "Wal, we'll be ready."

The next morning, Tex slid off his stool at the Chinaman's, after washing down a plate of flapjacks and corn syrup with draughts of black coffee. He sauntered up the courthouse steps.

Sheriff Cummings stood by his office window, gazing out upon the quiet street. He could have pitched a rock through the barred glass windows of the bank, set on the opposite corner. Even though the rising sun already glinted on the squat, square windows of the hotel across the way, few stirred. A wagon was backed up outside the mercantile store and a teamster piled sacks of flour beneath the wooden awning. Yawning, a swamper wearily washed the dusty windows of The Last Chance. A lonesome dark-featured rider lounged against the entrance of the hotel, arms folded, hat brim tilted low, smoking a cigarette.

"All primed for trouble?" queried Tex, joining the shiny-domed sheriff at the window. Cummings nodded.

"Ef you guess right, the gang's all primed f'r boothill."

"I ain't copperin' my bet," returned Tex grimly. "Look at that jasper yonder." He nodded toward the solitary rider. "He's keepin' cases on the bank, name of Cherokee."

As the sun mounted higher, Hanging Wells stirred and awoke. A janitor pushed back the heavy outer doors of the bank. Housewives, with floppy bonnets and big baskets, swept along the plankwalks with long skirts. Spring wagons and buggies rattled over the ruts. Men moved in and out of the bank doors, the zanzero's water wagon creaked from door to door. The daily life of Hanging Wells moved serenely along.

Restlessly Tex moved in and out of the courthouse and drifted from saloon to saloon, seeking sight of Scarface's crew, in vain. Even the dark-visaged lookout had disappeared. He stood sentry at the window of the sheriff's office and littered the floor with half-smoked cigarettes, ears ever attuned for the blare of six-guns that would prove his guess had hit the bull's-eye. But the hours, heat-laden and torpid, brought no action.

As though this day were no different from a thousand others, the sheriff moved methodically through his daily routine, with never a word to the newly-made deputy. The Texan knew that if his ideas miscarried, if Scarface had devised some new and ingenious plan for looting the gold, the finger of suspicion would point straight at him as an accomplice. That dried-up old tarantula of a sheriff would claim that he had tolled off the law while his pards made their getaway. He would have given his saddle to have been able to read the thoughts behind Cummings's guarded eyes.

As noon approached the bustle outside died down. Nerves on edge, Tex approached the window for the dozenth time. Another thirty minutes and the Copper Company's armed party would arrive and the gold would be transferred. Could he have guessed wrong?

"Hey!" His hoarse, excited whisper brought Cummings to his side. Five riders jogged along the street and wheeled to the hitch rail outside the Travelers Hotel. Casually they swung out of leather and loosely knotted their reins around the tie rail. One, a tall, thin fellow with dolorous features, lounged beneath the hotel awning, handy to the ponies' heads. Two others strolled across the road toward the bank. The remaining pair dogged them at a short distance.

"It's the gang!" breathed Tex, eyes riveted on Scarface and Kansas in the lead. The pair disappeared into the shadows of the bank entrance. The others followed. He swung toward the sheriff, standing cool and complacent, beside him. "Hell's due t' pop right now. Le's go!"

They were halfway down the courthouse steps when the shadowed quiet of the bank was shattered by the thunder of a forty-five. Another gun barked twice. The swinging door flew open and Scarface ducked out, a leather sack swinging from each hand. Kansas, guns gripped in both fists, pressed behind him. Then came Cherokee and Flatfoot, wheeling and shooting into the bank as they ran. As the door swung behind them, the blast of a shotgun within smashed the glass panels to a thousand fragments.

Across the road from the two lawmen, Wailing Willy leaped to the ponies' heads and tore the reins free from the rail.

Tex's right hand darted down. His swiveled holster jerked up, lanced fire. Willy spun around, slumped against a pony's rump and slid beneath its restless hooves. From the second story windows of the hotel, the courthouse roof, the doorway of the Western Mercantile Store on the opposite corner, a stream of lead laced the four scurrying men. The lash of rifle fire mingled with the roar of forty-fives.

Scarface staggered and fell flat, writhing feebly in the dust. Flatfoot dropped, dragged his big body upright, stood erect, twin guns spewing lead, then collapsed in a muddled heap. Cherokee darted for the shelter of the hotel, swerving like a startled rabbit, but a dozen slugs punched into his fast-moving form and he, too, plunged headlong. Only Kansas remained. Seemingly lead-proof, the wiry gunman bent, snatched up the sacks of gold with one hand, swerved from side to side. His gun spat red as he hit for the ponies. From the courthouse steps, Tex could see the slug-stired dust spurting around the solitary figure of the dodging gunman, like hail splattering a placid lake, but still they could not bring him down.

The bandits' ponies were loose. One bolted, the others milled and nickered, panic-stricken by the roar of gunfire and whine of lead. The gunnie grabbed one and swung into leather. Bending low, he drove home the steel. Frantically, the animal, eyes white-rimmed and tail streaming, shot past the courthouse with drumming hooves.

CHAPTER 6

With calm deliberation the sheriff leveled his six-gun as the pony carrying the lone survivor of the Scarface gang flashed past. Before he tripped the trigger, flame tipped Kansas's iron and Tex heard a choking gasp from the lawman. The Texan grabbed at his falling body, but he flopped forward out of reach. Bumping heavily from step to step, his body rolled to the foot of the stairway and came to a sprawling rest across the plankwalk.

Tex triggered into the dust plume that boiled high behind the threshing hooves of the bandit's pony. With a shrill scream the animal reared high, pawing the air. The little gunman stuck to leather like a leech, pounding the pony down with his clubbed gun. Despite his frantic efforts, the stricken animal slowly toppled backward. Tex caught a glimpse of the rider feverishly kicking free of the stirrups before the pony crashed to the ground and was blotted out by swirling dust.

Hand gripping the butt of his smoking gun, the Texan ran out into the road. Kansas was stretched out beside the body of his pony. The two sacks of gold lodged in a deep rut, where they had dropped from his limp hand. As Tex approached, he stirred, sat up and stared around with dazed eyes.

"By Gawd, you got more lives than a doggone

49

polecat!" growled Tex, kicking the killer's gun out of reach. He grabbed the gold, hoisted the half-stunned Kansas to his feet, steered him toward the jail.

The dust has scarcely settled before excited citizens poured out of doorways and alleys and milled around the still forms of the four dead bandits, surveying their slack features and staring eyes with morbid curiosity. Two men toted Sheriff Cummings's sagging form into the shade of the hotel awning.

Tex packed the gold up to the office. Cutting the leather thong that secured a sack, he spilled the contents in a shining, clinking cascade onto the desk top. Then he yelled out of the window for Plug Hawkins and Winters, his fellow deputies.

Five minutes later he pushed through the eagerly questioning crowd toward the bank. Paul Heinemann, the manager, clean-shaven features white and a shotgun gripped tightly in both hands, met him as he crunched over the shattered glass in the lobby.

"Where's the gold?" he demanded in an anxious voice.

"In the office," returned Tex shortly.

"Thank heavens!" breathed Heinemann. "And I called Dan an old woman for worrying about a holdup! Those damned desperadoes stick at nothing. Any prisoners?"

"One," returned Tex shortly, "and he'll swing ef the sheriff dies."

Doc Hoskins, a fussy little sparrow of a man with snapping eyes and a manner to match, was bending over Cummings, surrounded by an absorbed group, when Tex emerged from the bank.

He elbowed through to the sheriff's side. The medico was cleaning and bandaging a bullet hole in the old lawman'a chest. Red foam flecked Cummings's lips, but his eyes were as flinty as ever.

"We got him, Dan!" said Tex quietly.

The sheriff's wrinkled features twisted in a grin. "Nice work, Tex!" Then they packed his lank form through the hotel lobby, buzzing with excited guests like a disturbed beehive, up the threadbare carpet of the stairway, to the quiet of a room above.

Ten minutes later, when the Concha Copper Company's spring wagon and its mounted escort clattered through town, no signs of the frustrated holdup remained save smashed windows where the cornered killers had flung lead at the ringing rifles, and the ragged splinters of glass edging the panels of the bank door. The flies buzzed over the remnants of four dead bandits in a horse barn behind the mercantile store. Side by side they lay, gunbelts still buckled around their stiffening bodies, awaiting their last trip—to boothill.

In mid-afternoon a ragged Mexican boy brought Tex a summons to the wounded sheriff's side.

Deep-set eyes militant, propped up in a squeaky iron bed, Cummings's resemblance to an old baldheaded eagle was more marked than ever. Sitting around, on the bed and in chairs, were Paul Heinemann, Ted Barlow, the express agent, Jim McDonald, owner of the Western Mercantile Store and Monte Moreland, foreman of the Box-C.

Tex knuckled the closed door, pushed it open, and stepped into the stuffy little box of a room, with its faded square of carpet and cracked water pitcher set on the wash stand.

His eyes sought the bed, met the sheriff's unblinking gaze.

"How's tricks?" he inquired.

"Thet snap-shootin' galoot punched a hole in
my lungs." Cummings's voice was faint, his
seamed forehead glistened with sweat. "It ain't the
first chunk of lead I've stopped and it won't be the
last. I'll be around!"

"Tevis!" broke in Heinemann, the bank manager.

The Texan regarded him with puzzled eyes, then
smiled faintly. "They call me Tex!"

"Well, Tex, the sheriff's out of action for a few
weeks and we need a good man to tote his star. He
nominates you and," he waved a white, manicured
hand around the room, "we concur."

"You ain't speakin' f'r the Box-C, Heinemann!"
A well-remembered voice, deep and vibrant,
tightened every muscle in Tex's loose-jointed
frame. He swung around to face the taunting eyes
of Monte Moreland. The Box-C foreman's big
form was negligently spread over a chair, tilted
back against the wall. He grinned wolfishly at the
bleak hostility in the Texan's eyes and casually
touched a match to his cigarette.

"I know this hairpin," he continued, expelling a
mouthful of smoke. "We run him off Box-C range.
I'll gamble he threw in with thet Scarface outfit.
They sent him t' town t' case the joint and he
crossed 'em. Reckon thet five thousand dollar reward looked plumb good. He tips off Dan and you
boys clean 'em up f'r the yellow bastard." He bared
strong teeth at the tight-lipped Texan. "You're
outa luck, mister. The Concha Copper Company

put up thet money and they hadn't taken over the payroll."

Fists knotted, Tex plunged toward the mocking figure of the high-cheeked foreman. Heinemann thrust hastily between the pair, while Jim McDonald, a craggy Scotsman, and Ted Barlow, wiry and alert, hung onto the raging Texan.

"Monte!" said the bank manager brusquely. "The Box-C may rod the range, but it isn't running Hanging Wells—yet! We believe Tex is on the square. You can iron out your personal differences elsewhere."

Moreland spat derisively. "You'll change yore tone when I wise the Colonel up!"

"Hey!" croaked Cummings from the bed. "Howcome the Colonel swore Tex was ridin' line f'r the Box-C afore he come t' town?"

"Why ask me?" snarled Moreland, rising.

"Ain't you foreman?"

"Thet galoot was never on the Box-C payroll."

"Do you mean to say that the Colonel was lying?" asked Heinemann suavely.

The foreman swung toward the door. "Reckon the Colonel kin speak f'r hisself. I still say the county won't stand f'r no sulkin' nester as sheriff." His eyes glowered into Tex's. "Be seein' yuh, feller!" He stepped outside, slamming the door behind him.

The old sheriff's dry voice broke the silence that followed the jingle of the belligerent foreman's spurs down the corridor. "Monte's due t' stub his toe; them Box-C rannies act like they own the blasted Valley. Scared t' go ahead, Tex?"

"How about Hawkins and thet other deputy,

Winters? I only been around two-three days."

Cummings shook his head. "They're good men in a tight place but they don't fit the saddle. Paul, Jim and Ted," he nodded around, "are agreed yo're the man we need. Thet damned Box-C Apache don't count."

Tex shrugged. "Suits me!"

"And I intend to recommend to the bank's directors that they award you one thousand dollars," said Heinemann. "According to Dan, you most certainly earned it."

Plug Hawkins, bulky and slow-witted as a bull, eyed the sheriff's star on Tex's shirt without comment. "It was Dan's idea," explained the young Texan.

"Then it's okay by me," rumbled Plug. "But it don't look like yuh got enough wrinkles on your horns t' rod Dan's job."

"How's the prisoner doin?"

"Who cares a cuss?" yawned the jailor. "He'll hang up t' dry. Stray bullet croaked a guy in the store. Guess I'll lubricate. So long!"

For a while the young sheriff sat in deep thought, then he lifted the keys of the jail off a hook and descended into the basement of the courthouse. Kansas, apparently none the worse for his fall, hunkered against the rear of the cell, as silent and watchful as a caged cougar.

Sheriff and prisoner eyed each other through the bars.

"Reckon yuh know yore neck's due t' be stretched?" said Tex.

"What's it t' you?" snarled the wiry killer.

"It don't mean a damn thing." Tex's voice was

brittle. "What would yuh do ef yuh had a gun?"

"Gut-shoot you!" came the swift rejoinder. "Wish t' Gawd we'd plugged yuh last night."

Tex slipped an empty gun from beneath his waistband and pitched it through the bars. "I'm givin' yuh a chance, Kansas, t' bluff out with thet. And no rough stuff, or I'll cut yuh down afore you hit the plankwalk."

The bandit made no move to retrieve the weapon that thudded on the earth floor. Bleakly suspicious, his eyes darted from the gun to Tex's tall form.

"Takin' a leaf from the rurales' book?" he sneered. "Figger I'll talk ef I come t' trial, eh? Easier t' plug me makin' a break. Well, I ain't bitin'!"

"Kansas," said Tex evenly, "I jest as soon see you swing, you blasted little blacksnake! But I gotta debt t' pay. When we run off that Box-C herd my hoss busted his laig in a badger hole and I was set afoot. Woulda been cut down, but you reined up and carried me double. The other skunks split the breeze. This is where we even up—next time, come a-shootin'!"

With that he turned and left, locking the outer door behind him.

It was long past supper when Winters, a bony-faced deputy with rank hair and unsmiling lips, drifted into the office after making his rounds.

"Ain't seen Plug tote no chow downstairs," said Tex idly. "Thet prisoner's guts must be shrinkin'!"

Winters glanced at the key peg. "Say, the keys ain't here. Reckon he's down below." There was an uneasy note in his sharp voice.

"Let's go see!" suggested Tex.

Together they strode down the dark passage. Winters kicked metal with his boot. He groped on the floor, fished up the missing keys. With an oath he broke into a run, thudded down the stairway, Tex at his heels.

Through the heavy jail door a muffled shouting percolated. Winters swung it open. Tex picked a match from his hatband, touched it to the wick of the bracketed lamp.

Plug Hawkins was caged in the Kansan's cell. Voice hoarse with long shouting, he shook the steel door with impotent rage.

"Thet dogblasted wildcat packed a hidden gun," he grated. "Threw down on me and skeedaddled."

Half dozing, Tex slumped in the sheriff's swivel chair, waiting for the exodus of drunks when the saloons closed at midnight. Reaction from the strain and excitement of the day—the anticipated holdup, the fracas with the Scarface gang, the Box-C foreman's accusation, Kansas's getaway—found him worn out, mentally and physically.

Stifling a yawn, he lazily turned his head as quick, light steps pattered on the planked corridor outside. Snapped into wakefulness by quick surprise, he jumped to his feet as Kathryn O'Keefe flung the door open and dashed breathlessly into the room.

At sight of him, she gasped with relief and stood panting, cheeks rosy with exertion and eyes sparkling with excitement.

Her breast rose and fell spasmodically beneath the tight dress that outlined her graceful figure, as she strove to speak.

"Set down, ma'am!" said Tex kindly. "Jest take it easy—trouble at The Double Eagle?"

Kathryn found her voice at last. "Trouble!" she

echoed. "I'll say there's trouble—for you." Her voice rose high with anxiety and indignation. "There's two scoundrelly Mexicans at the bar, half drunk. They're plannin' to kill you!"

"Wal, I ain't dead yet," drawled the Texan. "These Mexicans, now, are they makin' their intentions public?"

"No!" The girl was calmer now. "They're boasting, one to the other, in Spanish. I understand their talk. Someone gave them a hundred dollars to kill you—the sneaky cutthroats!"

"Who?" asked Tex quickly.

He glimpsed a quick change of expression in her dark eyes, sensed an almost imperceptible pause before she answered, "I don't know."

"You sure?"

"Are you doubting my word, after trying to save your worthless hide, Tex Tevis?" she demanded angrily.

"No, ma'am, I'm shore grateful." He reached for his Stetson. "Reckon I'll mosey down t' the saloon—"

He abruptly grabbed the girl's shoulder, placed his hand over her mouth and hustled her into a closet that held slickers and a gun-rack. Scarcely had he pushed the door shut behind her, when there came a timid tap at the office door.

At Tex's shouted summons, the door eased open gently and a pock-faced Mexican, big sombrero clutched in brown hands and greasy tilma hanging from his shoulders, slid in with an oily smile.

"Señor!" he whined. "I am veery sad. My cousin and I breeng mucho gold back from the mine. When I got to cantina to take wan dreenk, a beeg thief keel my cousin and steal the gold. You come to our casa, muy pronto? Mebbeso, we catch keeler?"

Tex wrinkled his nose at the stench of rotgut.

"Your cousin in the jackel—dead?"

The Mexican nodded and sniffed. "Beeg thief keel him!" he moaned.

"Lemme look at him! Le's get goin', Pancho!"

CHAPTER 7

Gathering his ragged cloak around him, the Mexican padded along the shadowed plankwalk in soundless zapatos. Alert for treachery, Tex strode behind the muffled form.

At the end of the business section, where Main Street abruptly petered out into a wide trail, the plankwalk terminated. The Mexican angled off through the sparse brush and plunged into the crowded chaos that was the Mexican quarter. By the wan light of the stars, he swiftly threaded through a motley of adobes, strewn over the flat. From one floated the plaintive music of a guitar, from another issued a stream of voluble Spanish as a woman scolded a squawking child, but the hour was late and most of the squat shadowy dwellings were darkened and quiet.

All a sudden the guide jerked to a stop and turned excitedly, grasping the Texan's arm. He pointed to the gray outline of an adobe straight ahead. The door was ajar.

"Eet es la casa!" He crossed himself. "My cousin, he ees dead. May the blessed saints receive his soul!"

"No one else inside?" Tex's narrowed eyes swept around. Nothing moved in the vicinity save a wandering cur, nosing among the offal that richly scented the night air.

"Que mas? Who else, save the remains of my poor cousin."

"Go ahead!"

The Mexican shrank away. "Por dios! Señor, I dare not. My cousin, ee ees de—" The sheriff's left hand shot out and fastened on the Mexican's narrow shoulder. In a trice he twisted the protesting man around. The cold muzzle of his gun nudged the back of the guide's neck. "Shut thet trap," he grated, "and march ahead. One squawk and I'll blow yore conk right off'n yore shoulders."

Impelled by Tex's strong arm, the Mexican reluctantly shuffled toward the gray adobe. As they approached the door, he squealed like a stuck rabbit and struggled desperately to twist free. The sheriff clouted him with his clubbed gun. Half insensible, he staggered ahead, held erect by the relentless Texan.

They reached the doorway. Tex stretched out a long leg, kicked the door open, pushed the tottering Mexican into the darkened entrance and threw himself to one side. As he jumped he was deafened by the roar of a six-gun, thunderous in the confined space of the adobe. A quavering shriek tore the guide's throat as he flung backward and collapsed, clawing the ground convulsively. Through the darkness came excited exclamations from neighboring adobes, the jabber of aroused sleepers, the barking of dogs, whining of children, but no one ventured into the open.

Bending low, Tex plunged through the doorway, into the black obscurity. Again a gun spurted scarlet and a slug whined over his head. By the flash, he glimpsed a figure crouching by the rear wall. His own iron lanced red as he threw himself headlong on the bare earth floor and rolled sideways. Silence engulfed the darkened room. Eyes straining, ears acute, Tex endeavored to locate the would-be assassin. Beside him, the rising moon projected a faint oblong of pale light upon the ground. Weighted by tension, the seconds dragged, but not a sound disturbed the deep silence that impinged upon the Texan's tensed nerves until they were as taut as violin strings. Soundlessly he eased a cartridge from his gun-belt and tossed it to his left. A gun blared with a suddenness that told him his were not the only tensed nerves, as it tinkled upon the ground. Plain in the powder flash, he saw the swarthy features and stooping form of a Mexican, not ten paces distant. His iron spat fire and thunder—once, twice, three times. Again darkness cloaked the adobe, hacked by the choking moans of a man in mortal agony.

Tex wormed over against the wall to his right, then inched forward, cocked gun gripped in his fist. The moaning became fainter—died away. Wary of a trick, the sheriff extended his left arm toward the source of the sound. His groping fingers touched a boot. He lifted the outstretched leg—it dropped limply. Swiftly changing position, he struck a match. The faint flame revealed a huddled body, with gaping mouth and staring eyes. A gun with ivory grips lay beside it—the Mexican's cousin, if it were his cousin, was in truth dead, very dead.

Tex straightened and strode out of the acrid air of the smoke-filled adobe. The guide's body was sprawled across the threshold. Tex dragged the remains inside and closed the door. Vague figures flitted through the gloom, but no one molested him as he hit for the center of town.

It was a vast relief to walk through the broad shafts of light streaming from saloons and rub shoulders with gray-shirted punchers after the eerie darkness and ominous quiet of the Mexican quarter. He pushed through the batwings of The Double Eagle. The usual throng hunched around card tables and crooked elbows at the bar. As he emerged into the yellow glare of the oil lamps, he saw Kathryn O'Keefe's head jerk around nervously. Her eyes focused upon him with quick relief, then she busied herself beside her thick-set, ruddy-haired father pushing drinks across the bar.

"Gimme a slug—I shore earned it," said the Texan, setting a foot on the brass rail.

"What happened?" she inquired eagerly.

"Them Mexicans won't spend that dinero—never." His grin was humorless.

"You—killed them!" she gasped.

"You ain't mournin' them skunks?"

"Well," she hesitated, "was it really necessary?"

"Yuh don't palaver with rattlesnakes," he replied grimly. "And I'm shore thankin' you, ma'am, f'r the tip-off."

Her face straightened. "I believe in upholding the law."

"I figgered thet maybe it was personal regard." She tossed her head.

"You flatter yourself, Tex Tevis! Besides, who would associate with a girl who spends her time in a low-down saloon?"

"It ain't exactly elevatin'," he drawled.

Kathryn's cheeks blazed. She checked a swift retort on her lips, banged a glass on the bar and moved stiffly away.

"Hey, ma'am!" hailed the Texan. Lips prim,

dark eyes flashing, she returned.

"Did I tell yuh, ma'am, that when you're riled you look as pretty as a heart flush?"

"You ma'am me again," she threatened fiercely, "and I'll bust a bottle right on your thick skull."

"Wine is a mocker, strong drink is raging and whosoever is deceived thereby is not wise." Preacher Paul's deep-throated roar at the doorway brought every head in the saloon around. Tawdry frock coat thrown back, bony hands upon his hips, gun sagging at his side, the Preacher's accusing blue eyes met the concerted gaze of the patrons, some contemptuous, a few amused, the majority derisive.

"Yo're in the wrong stall, bible-puncher! Go preach t' the wimmenfolk," bawled a raw-boned rider.

"The wrong stall, you befuddled fool!" bellowed Paul. "I see a score of souls hell-bound for eternal fire."

"Git out, long-hair, or I'll toss yuh out!" threatened the rider, his voice thick. Swaying slightly, he advanced upon bow legs toward the whiskered Preacher.

"He who meddles with the Lord's messenger shall verily be cast into outer darkness," warned Paul, eyes blazing.

Unheeding, the puncher, bemused by whiskey, dove at the Preacher's massive form. As quick on his feet as a big cat, the Preacher sidestepped, raised his boot as the attacker stumbled past, threshing the air, placed it squarely against the seat of his pants and thrust him through the swinging doors, out into the night.

A roar of laughter greeted the Preacher's adroit

defense. It was stilled as the discomfited puncher burst through the batwings, launched himself at his opponent's back and clung desperately, arms locked around Paul's bull neck.

Nowise ruffled, the Preacher bent forward in a swift arc, tossed the pummeling, kicking rider over his head, gathered him up in his mighty arms as he crashed to the floor and unconcernedly threw him back from whence he came.

"The wicked shall be vanquished and truth shall prevail!" he thundered. "Now listen, unbelievers!" Awed by the display of physical strength, the motley crowd of gamblers, punchers, townsmen, stood silent. "With the aid of the good Lord I can out-fight, out-wrestle or out-shoot any black-souled unbeliever in this saloon. If any disbelieve me, let him stand forth or forever hold his peace."

"Betcher a ten-spot I kin out-shoot yuh, Preacher!" challenged a wiry, hard-eyed hombre.

"The Lord kin use that ten dollars," roared Paul. "Set up a mark!"

A somber-faced gambler stuck the ace of spades on a nail protruding from the farther wall. Side bets flew freely as the patrons eagerly made a lane for the one-spot to the center of the saloon, a distance of twenty paces.

The challenger steadied himself, thumbed back the hammer of his gun and slowly threw down on the mark. With a roar, the weapon bucked. A rush of men bunched around the card. The slug had punched a neat hole, the width of a dollar from the pip.

"Good shooting, friend, but not good enough," rumbled Paul. With practiced ease, his brawny gun swept down. The long-barreled Colt he toted thundered. Excited expletives ripped from the spectators' lips as they crowded the card—the black center spot had disappeared.

"I'd shore hate t' match cutters with you, mister," mumbled the chagrined rider, as he fumbled in his pants pocket.

"In all things the Lord is a conqueror," intoned the Preacher sonorously, blowing the smoke from the barrel of his gun. He bestowed the wager in a leather purse and proceeded to unroll a poster which he abstracted from one of the capacious pockets in the tail of his frock coat. Ringed by curious men, he spiked the poster over the perforated ace of spades. Crudely lettered, it read:

GRAND GOSPEL MEETING
Sunday next
at 10 a.m.
in the
Double Eagle Saloon
by the
courtesy of
Patrick O'Keefe

———

Collection for Dan Cummings's Wife

———

REPENT YE SINNERS!

"Say, Preacher!" cracked a whiskery puncher. "The souls of these gents done shriveled up and blown away long afore you hit town."

"Though your sins be as scarlet they shall be as white as snow," intoned Paul. His piercing eyes swept the circle of silent men. "Whether ye be hellbound or not, come, praise the good Lord and drop a dollar in the plate for Dan's wife. She has nothin' but a crippled husband, a frame house and ten acres of alkali flat. St. Peter's got a powerful long memory and here's yuhr chance to grease your way through the Pearly Gates."

Tex eased toward the door. When the burly Preacher breezed through the batwings, he fell in beside him. "How'm I doin', Paul?" He indicated the badge.

"Tolerable, my son, but be not puffed up, for thine enemies encompass thee."

"Yo're tellin' me!" grunted the Texan. "Some sidewinder dropped a coupla Mexicans a hundred dollars t' put my light out."

"And they failed!" ejaculated the Preacher triumphantly. "The Lord preserveth all them that love him, but the wicked will he destroy."

"I helped some!" objected Tex.

"The Lord chooseth his own instruments, but it don't hinder none to tote a fast gun. May peace be unto you!" Paul loosed the reins of his mule, stepped across its razor back and ambled away into the night. Tex gazed thoughtfully after the strange character. "Slickest gun hand I seen in a coon's age," he murmured to himself. "Whereinhell did he git the practice?"

Heinemann was restlessly pacing the office when the sheriff returned. The bank manager swiveled like a startled cat when Tex pushed open the door.

"They got the payroll!" he burst out.

"Who?" asked Tex incredulously.

"How would I know?" Heinemann's voice was sharp-edged with mingled anxiety and anger. "One gang staged a fake attack on the wagon ten miles out and drew the escort away in pursuit. They lost the crafty coyotes in the hills. When they returned to the wagon there was nothing left but five murdered men. The gold was gone."

"So the Scarface gang was lone wolves, stagin' their own snatch!" Tex rolled a smoke, forehead knitted. "Looks like there's a long-headed jasper roddin' them road agents. Any tracks?"

"The bandits scattered and disappeared into the Barrens—as usual," returned Heinemann bitterly.

"Figger they'll spend the dinero?"

"What if they do?" asked the bank manager impatiently. "We can identify banknotes by their numbers, but who can swear to a gold coin?"

"I kin!" said Tex quietly.

"Identify gold—you're crazy!"

"Set down! You're as figgety as a cat on a hot stove." Tex good-naturedly pushed the fuming banker into a straight-backed chair. "Now lissen! I had the boys nick the edge of every gold piece in them sacks. Send the word around—quiet like. We'll grab the first guy who passes thet payroll cash and we'll sweat a confession outa the bustard."

CHAPTER 8

A stuttering salvo of shots, punctuated by wild "yippees," brought Tex to the window of his office at the jump. As the sun sank in scarlet splendor behind the Smokies, a bunch of Box-C punchers swept down the street. The watching sheriff caught a glimpse of Moreland's coppery features in their midst and had a swift premonition of trouble.

An hour later, Winters pushed open the door. "Them Box-C boys are raisin' hell in The Double Eagle. O'Keefe tried t' get his gal out, but thet crazy Apache foreman swore they'd burn down the joint ef she didn't serve drinks."

"Figger they're liable t' misuse her?" The Texan's voice was taut.

"Them ranahans are liable t' do anything when they get lickered up."

Without further word, Tex buckled on his gun-belt and reached for his Stetson.

"Want I should round up Plug and go with yuh?" inquired the deputy.

"Nope, three ain't much more use than one. You hold down the office."

"They's a dozen Box-C waddies and they're liable t' throw lead."

"I'm playin' this hand," returned Tex shortly.

He descended the courthouse steps and moved along the darkening street.

Outside The Double Eagle a cluster of interested onlookers pressed their noses against the windows. Within, the off-key piano tinkled through the shouting of the roistering riders. A woman's shriek ripped the air and was smothered in a roar of laughter.

Tex's pace quickened. He shouldered through the batwings.

The pianist, an elderly townsman who clerked in the mercantile store by day, pounded frantically at the ivories. One drunken waddy prodded him with a six-gun, another solemnly trickled the contents of a beer bottle over his graying head.

Pat O'Keefe, belligerent jaw set and a bottle in his fist, battled two punchers behind the bar. By the far wall, ringed by guffawing riders, his daughter, hair disheveled and eyes blazing, fought like a wildcat to escape the encircling arms of Moreland.

"I got a five-spot thet sez yuh can't kiss her!" yelled a waddy, as the girl's crooked fingers dug red tracks on the foreman's dusky face. Moreland grabbed the girl's hand and forced her body backward with a triumphant grin, one arm around her waist. She twisted her head sideways to avoid his mocking lips ... a hard fist thudded into the foreman's ear. He staggered under the impact of the blow. The girl wrenched free from his relaxed grip and fled through the welter of upturned tables and empty bottles that littered the sawdust.

Moreland steadied himself, swung around with an oath to face his assailant. At sight of Tex he grinned, dark eyes malevolent.

"Doggone ef it ain't our tinhorn sheriff! Wanta trade lead, mister, or ain't you got the guts?"

"I'll even the matter up later," returned the Tex-

an coolly. "Right now I'm takin' you in, Moreland, f'r disturbin' the peace."

Hands on hips, the foreman roared with
laughter. "Hear thet, boys?" he shouted, as the
Box-C riders gathered around. "The sheriff's jug-
gin' me!" His voice grew harsh. "Why, yuh
swaybacked sheep-herder, we'll tear yuh in little
pieces and feed yuh t' the coyotes. Yow-l-l-l." His
voice rose in a wild shriek. "We're curly-tailed
wolves and it's our night t' howl."

Tex backed against the wall, eyes shuttling from
the dark features of the foreman to the circling
Box-C waddies. He knew cow hands, and he knew
that the Box-C bunch, reckless and well-liquored,
were in a mood to start any deviltry. Even if their
foreman had been a willing prisoner, it would have
been harder to take him out of that saloon than to
have snatched a fat calf from a circle of famishing
wolves.

"Take it easy, boys!" he warned. "I got deputies
outside."

"Bring 'em in!" challenged Moreland. A wicked
grin curved his lips. "Grab him, boys! Let's send
him home in his birthday suit!"

With yelps of joy, the flushed Box-C riders
charged toward the tensed figure of the sheriff. He
was fingering his gun when a mighty roar brought
them up short. "Wine is a mocker! It turneth man
into a jackass and is an abomination unto the
Lord. What is this madness?"

The Preacher kicked overturned tables and upset
chairs aside as he advanced from the doorway with
long strides. His big paw descended upon the
shoulder of a stumpy, bow-legged puncher. With
apparent ease, he gripped the slack of the fellow's

pants with his free hand, hoisted the struggling
form high and threw him, with threshing arms and
legs, into the pack of men. As they broke in confusion, he grabbed two more, slapped their heads
together with a resounding crash and tossed their
reeling forms aside. One waddy stabbed for his
gun. Moreland checked his arm. "Lay off!" he
growled. "Thet bible-puncher's death on the
draw."

The Preacher stepped up beside the Texan, blue
eyes focused on the disorganized and chastened
punchers. "The Lord smote the Philistines," he intoned, "and delivered his Chosen People. Were
you about to make an arrest, Sheriff?"

Tex jerked his head toward the glowering
Moreland. "Yep, I'm a-goin' t' jug that jasper."

"Then go to it! If any man interferes, the lion of
Judah will verily tear him limb from limb." With
the deep-voiced declaration he stepped toward the
Box-C riders. Unwillingly, they backed, growling
like wolves retreating from the kill.

The sheriff turned to Moreland, standing, with
clouded features, alone. "Are yuh goin' quiet, mister?"

"F'r you!" Contempt laced the foreman's bitter
words.

The Texan unbuckled his gun-belt. "You'll go ef
I have t' pack yuh." He tossed the gun-belt on the
floor. Moreland's thudded beside it.

The discomfited punchers, held in check by the
threat of the Preacher's massive arms and the magic of his draw, forgot their resentment as their eyes
focused on the two antagonists, circling warily,
fists bunched, bitter animosity lined on grim,
watchful faces. They saw stark hatred in More-

land's smoldering eyes, a hatred which was
reflected on the Texan's somber features. Neither
man had the advantage of height, but the foreman
bulked big against Tex's lean form.

Swift as a striking hawk, Moreland drove in,
arms pounding like pistons. Tex sidestepped the
headlong rush, but his left foot slipped on a patch
of wet floor. Momentarily, he lost balance and the
foreman's fist smashed into his nose. It spurted
red. Blood streaming over his chin, he swayed
backward. The Box-C waddies yelled as Moreland
bored in for a quick kill, but the Texan leaped forward, flung long arms around his opponent and
clung like a saddle-burr, pinning the raging
foreman's arms down. In vain, the maddened
Moreland fought to free himself and bring his
smashing fists into play, but the sheriff held on,
face numbed by the force of the blow and head
reeling.

Slowly, the Texan's head cleared. He relaxed his
grasp, hammered a quick left-right into Moreland's belly and jumped clear. Gasping, the foreman plunged after him like a maddened bull. Tex
swung sideways. His right shot out and took
Moreland beside the jaw as the foreman was carried past by the impetus of his headlong rush.
Moreland staggered, pivoted and bored in again,
seeking to overwhelm his quick-footed opponent in
a shower of punches.

Dodging, ducking and feinting, the Texan
avoided his bulky antagonist's blind rushes, but
continually his long right flicked out, damaging
and tormenting the hard-breathing Moreland.

"Why don't yuh fight like a man, not a blasted
jackrabbit?" gasped the foreman. His right eye was

closing, blood trickled from the corner of his mouth. The Texan was unmarked, save for the blood smeared from his damaged nose. At Moreland's words he darted in, feinted with his left and snapped Moreland's head back with a straight right. Before the angered foreman could retaliate, he had slipped back out of reach.

Again he sidestepped and slipped a succession of blind rushes, while the watching riders howled in derision. The Preacher stood with folded arms, beard outthrust, eyes shining above his curved nose, like a prophet of old. Flattened noses made white blobs against the saloon windows, as an ever-growing crowd of spectators eyed the battle. Behind the bar, alone and forgotten, stood Kathryn and her father, the Irishman yelling triumphantly every time Tex's fists thudded home, the girl wide-eyed and silent.

Moreland was slowing. His wide mouth sagged as he sucked air into heaving lungs, his legs and arms seemed weighted. The Texan, circling, slipping in and out, gave him no rest. The pecking right had half closed his other eye; he spat out a tooth. Then the sheriff changed his tactics. Feet firmly planted, chin tucked in, he stood his ground before Moreland's lumbering rush. Heads lowered, arms swinging like sledges, they fought toe to toe. The riders' derisive yells were stilled. They watched with tight lips as the slugging fists of the two hard-breathing, bitter-eyed fighters sank into each other's torsos with flat, fleshy thuds. Not a blow was parried. The onlookers sensed that it could not last long; one or the other must go down before the pounding onslaught.

Tex grunted as a fist clipped his jaw, reeled,

quickly regained his balance, bored in again with a
volley of short-arm jabs that rocked the panting
Moreland. The foreman staggered. A swift up-
percut took him beneath the chin. With a crash he
went down. Chest rising and falling, face and shirt
besmeared with blood, the sheriff stood above him.
Moreland swayed to his feet, lowered his head and
charged blindly. Tex snapped his head up with a
left hook that loosened his jaw. As he teetered
upon his heels, eyes staring, the sheriff slung a right
to his jaw, every ounce of strength in his bruised
body behind it. Again the foreman went down—
like a pole-axed steer. His limp form sprawled mo-
tionless across the sawdust.

"How hath the mighty fallen!" intoned the
Preacher. "The Lord hath girded thee with
strength, my son, but you took a mighty long
chance slugging it out; his weight was against yuh."

Tex wiped the salty blood from his mouth with
his bandanna, buckled on his belt and picked up
Moreland's gun-belt. The form on the floor stirred,
painfully struggled to a sitting position and gazed
around in bewilderment.

Tex grabbed him under the armpits and he staggered erect. Glassy-eyed, he suffered the lawman to
lead him toward the batwings.

Trailed by an open-mouthed throng, feasting its
eyes on the bloodied, disheveled figures, the sheriff
and his prisoner moved slowly toward the
courthouse.

At noon, the following day, a messenger brought
Tex an urgent request from Heinemann to step
across to the bank.

The gaps left by the mashed panels in the door had been boarded up, pending arrival of fresh window glass. An elderly man in shirt sleeves stood behind the cashier's wicket. At a desk in the rear, a lanky, pale-faced youth, with greased hair and neat mustache, bent over a ledger. To the right, the door of Heinemann's private office hung wide open.

Tex sauntered in and closed the door behind him. The bank manager sat behind a flat-topped desk. He swept aside a litter of documents as the sheriff hooked a chair up to the desk, and slid open a drawer. Upon the desk top he arranged three neat piles of gold coin.

"Payroll money?" inquired Tex, with quick interest.

Heinemann nodded. "Forty ten-dollar gold pieces, every one nicked." He tossed a coin to the sheriff. Tex ran his forefinger over the milled edge and nodded.

"Who turned 'em in?"

"You'd never guess," replied Heinemann slowly.

"I ain't tryin'—is the jasper in town?"

"It's a woman—Pat O'Keefe's daughter."

"What!" gasped the Texan incredulously.

"She deposited the coins you see here, totaling four hundred dollars, in her savings account, not fifteen minutes ago."

"Reckon she took the coin in over the bar."

Heinemann shook his head. "Pat banks his receipts every morning at ten o'clock—as regular as a clock. Miss O'Keefe has her own account."

"But, dammit, thet gal ain't no thievin' road agent."

Heinemann shrugged well-tailored shoulders.

"I'm merely showing you the evidence. As sheriff, it's your duty to investigate and take any necessary action."

Tex pushed back his chair. "I figger thet there's a mix-up somewheres. The O'Keefe gal's on the square. I'll check and report back."

Brow furrowed, he moved toward the door. His thoughts flew back to Kathryn O'Keefe's hurried visit to warn him against the Mexican bush-whackers. He could have sworn she had lied when she denied knowledge of the man who had paid a hundred dollars for his death. Was she tied in with the payroll bandits? If so, how deep was she in?

CHAPTER 9

Dodging a freight wagon lumbering behind a string of toiling mules, Tex headed for The Double Eagle. Loitering Mexicans dozed in the shade of the plankwalk canopies, a scattering of riders hunkered against store fronts, mongrels nosed half-heartedly in the gutters. Plug Hawkins trudged toward him, fleshy features wilted. "Hot, ain't it, Tex?" he rumbled. "Say, I jest saw a hound dawg chasin' a jack-rabbit—they both *walked.*" The sheriff, absorbed in his mission, nodded abstractedly, while the burly deputy guffawed at his own wit.

Kathryn O'Keefe, in spotless shirtwaist and white apron, busied herself behind the bar of The Double Eagle. Four punchers, grouped around a table, were the only patrons. They drank warm beer and aimlessly flicked the pasteboards.

The girl's eyes sparkled at sight of Tex's loose-jointed figure. Before he reached the deserted bar, she reached for his favorite brand and poured a drink. "It's on the house," she smiled. In a softer tone, she added, "You're wonderful, Tex. That beast Moreland scared me plenty."

Silently he downed the bourbon and stood watching her with intent gaze. "Why, what's wrong?" she ejaculated, nervously patting the shimmering rope of copper hair coiled neatly around her head.

"The Concha Copper Company lost a pile of dinero in thet last holdup," he commented, without preamble.

"Well, what of it?"

"It was marked money." The sheriff's tone was matter-of-fact, but his narrowed eyes never left the girl's face.

Kathryn's eyes dropped before his scrutiny.

"Well?" The challenging retort was faint, almost a whisper.

"You banked forty ten-dollar gold pieces. That gold was payroll money. Where did yuh git it?"

"If you're accusin' me of—" she began heatedly.

"I'm accusin' you of nothin'," he barked. "I'm askin'."

Fumbling with a bar towel, she backed uncertainly. Tex leaned across the bar. His long arm shot out and his fingers curled around her wrist.

"Where did yuh git the dinero?" he repeated.

Angrily, the girl tried to twist free. "Take your big paw off my arm, Tex Tevis!" she bristled. "That tin star doesn't give you the right to manhandle me—even though I do serve behind a bar."

"Answer the question," he gritted, his hold tightening, "or I'll jug yuh, sure as shootin'; five men was murdered in that holdup."

She hesitated, eyes averted. "We took it in over the bar." He barely heard the low-voiced words.

"You're lyin'!"

With a quick wrench, the girl broke free, darted out of reach, snatched a sawed-off shotgun beneath the bar. Whirling, she cocked the twin triggers.

"You get out of here," she panted, "or I'll fill you so full of lead you'll sink in brine."

The Texan's cold eyes swept over her flushed features and blazing eyes. With an indifferent shrug of the shoulders he turned and walked slowly toward the batwings. In his heart, rankling suspicion mingled with bitter disappointment. During the few action-packed days he had spent in Hanging Wells the spunky, ruddy-haired daughter of Pat O'Keefe had come to mean more to him than he would admit to himself. Now she was linked with a dastardly bunch of killers; for she had lied, there was no doubt of that. Her father banked the cash that came over the bar himself. Fear had glimmered in her eyes when she learned the money was marked.

Gloomy and preoccupied, he almost collided with Pat O'Keefe himself as he thrust back the batwings. The thick-set Irishman slapped him jovially on the shoulder. "Shore, and I'm thankin' yez, Tex, for yore help in handlin' them scalpeens last evening."

"Tell me, Pat," the sheriff's voice was sharp. "Does Kathryn take money from the cash box?"

"Are yez calling my daughter a sneak thafe?" demanded O'Keefe indignantly.

"Pull in yore horns!" soothed Tex. "Could she have helped herself to, say, four hundred dollars the past day or so?"

"Yo're crazy with the heat!" snorted the other.

"Mebbe," rejoined the sheriff wearily, and strode away.

Scratching his close-cropped hair, O'Keefe stared after the long form with puzzled eyes. "Four hundred dollars," he muttered. "Holy Mither, the lad's loco, we ain't had a hundred dollar day f'r a month."

A girl's clear voice hailed the sheriff as he passed the drooping orange trees, neatly tubbed, that marked the entrance to the Travelers Hotel. Diana Cresswell tripped across the lobby, her cool beauty in refreshing contrast to the limp, perspiring forms of men slumped in the rockers around her.

"I just wanted to congratulate you—Tex." She lingered on the name. "Quite a jump from—well, you know"—her blue eyes twinkled—"to sheriff. And what did you do to poor Monte? When he rode in this morning he looked as though a mountain lion had mauled him."

"Resistin' arrest!" Tex smiled, too; it was hard to resist her infectious friendliness.

"I heard differently. The men say you two staged a terrific fist fight." She shivered delicately. "I wish I'd been there!"

"It warn't no place f'r a woman." With quickening of the pulse, he thought of Kathryn O'Keefe fighting to escape Moreland's embrace, then his eyes hardened as he remembered her perfidy.

"I love reckless men, fighting men," cooed Diana. "Monte was too masterful. I'm glad he was put in his place, especially by you."

Tex shuffled his feet uneasily. Not an eye in the lobby but was focused upon Diana Cresswell's flawless figure. Her father's wealth and power, added to her blond beauty, gave her a distinction that drew willing homage from every eligible male. But the Texan had had little contact with womanfolk. The girl's obvious flattery was pleasing, but mighty embarrassing.

He looked down into the blue depths of her eyes and hastily averted his gaze. Through the open door he glimpsed Kathryn O'Keefe, a solitary figure, hurrying along the plankwalk. The girl glanced into the lobby, absorbed the picture, jerked up her small chin, wheeled and retraced her footsteps.

Diana's curious eyes followed the sheriff's intent gaze.

"Isn't that the only woman bartender west of Chicago?" she asked lightly, a subtle disdain in her clear voice. "She's pretty, too, in a brazen sort of way."

Tex grunted, at a loss for words.

"Well, I really must be going. Come out to the ranch sometime—soon. I'm sure Dad would like you better if he really knew you."

With a graceful wave of her slim hand she crossed the lobby, superbly indifferent to the battery of masculine eyes. With mixed feelings, Tex hastily withdrew.

In the privacy of his office the sheriff glumly chewed a cigarette to pulp as he mulled over Kathryn O'Keefe's possible complicity in the payroll lootings. It was difficult to believe that the spirited daughter of the saloon keeper could have any connection with a gang of dastardly killers, yet the proof was plain. The four hundred dollars she banked was part of the loot. No other marked coin had been reported. How had the gold reached her hands? Was she a paid spy of the gang, acting as "eyes" for the bandits in Hanging Wells? The Texan's heart sank as he considered the implications. The idol he had cherished of the spunky, coppery-haired girl slowly crumbled to dust.

With a quick gesture of impatience, he spat out the sodden remnants of the smoke and slapped on his Stetson.

In the shadowed silence of the bank Heinemann was still sitting at his desk. His sharp eyes raised inquiringly to the sheriff, as the latter entered.

"Miss O'Keefe claims thet dinero came over the bar," said Tex abruptly.

The banker shook his head. "O'Keefe banks his take every day, as you know!"

"Wal, that's her story."

"Do you believe it?" shot Heinemann crisply.

The sheriff raised his shoulders. "Ain't no reason f'r the gal t' run with that bunch and there's no proof she does."

"Except the indisputable evidence."

"Ain't a jury in Concha County would convict her," persisted Tex doggedly. "Let it ride! First time she stubs her toe I'll grab her."

"You're sheriff," agreed the banker doubtfully. "It's amazing to find Miss O'Keefe involved, but sex should not provide immunity. I'm relying on you to see this thing through."

"I will." The sheriff's voice was grim. "Now," he added, yanking up a chair, "about the next shipment. We gotta git it through."

"What more can we do?" demanded Heinemann irately. "That last payroll would have been safe if those fool guards hadn't allowed themselves to be tolled away."

"How come it was held up?"

"For the gold, of course!" The banker looked sharply at the still-featured Tex.

"How come they knew the gold was aboard? The wagon comes in every day from the mine f'r mail and supplies, but it's never been held up except when it was packin' the payroll."

Heinemann's smooth forehead puckered. He leaned back in his chair, eyes keen with interest. His voice quickened.

"There's a leak!"

"Or a spy," said the Texan softly. "Let's fool him next time."

"What would you suggest we do?" Heinemann asked.

"Make up a dummy payroll and ship it on the wagon, with an armed guard. Then shoot the dinero along in a buggy, behind a coupla good ponies, mebbe an hour later. And don't let no one in on the switch outside the bank. No one, mister!"

"We assume a risk, sending the gold without escort, but it might work out," agreed Heinemann thoughtfully. "We'll try it. Anything to check these infamous holdups."

Again the spring wagon, behind four fast horses, rattled down Main Street to the bank, its heavily armed escort churning the dust behind.

While the watchful riders cautiously eyed the few curious onlookers, a wooden box was carried from the bank by its rope handles and dumped into the wagon bed. Sided by two shotgun guards and tailed by the jingling escort, the driver shook his team into a canter and the party whirled out of town.

An hour later, a buggy, to which was harnessed two snorting broncs, pulled quietly out the alley beside the bank and hit westward in the wake of the wagon. Barlow, the express agent, handled the ribbons.

Two miles out of town, where the wagon road curved through thickets of scrub oak, tipped red with new bursting leaves, the ponies of Tex and Winters grazed with loosened cinches, while the two lawmen hunkered beside the trail.

The distant snap of a whip and the shrill yelp of a raucous-voiced driver brought the pair to their feet.

The wagon swung into view through the tree trunks, trail dust swirling as the ponies' hooves clipped the powdery earth. Behind, in pairs, cantered the six riders, alert for action.

Tex stepped into the middle of the wagon road and held his hand high. Under the bleak eyes of the shotgun guards, he strode past the plunging ponies, fighting their bits, while the escorting riders wheeled around.

"Step down and rest awhile!" he ordered them curtly.

"This heah's the mine payroll," yelled the driver. "What's the play, Sheriff?"

"The payroll ain't due f'r an hour."

"Yo're loco!" The sweating driver fought his nervous team and glanced over his shoulder at the box in the wagon. "It's right heah!"

"Take a look!" Tex grinned at the perplexity on the faces around him.

A guard jumped into the wagon bed, pried open the box lid and hefted a small leather sack. With his sheath knife he cut the thong that bound the neck of the sack, plunged in his hand. A chorus of startled oaths ripped out as he displayed a handful of sand.

"Take it easy, boys, and rest yore saddles," advised Tex. "The dinero will be a-comin' along the trail in an hour."

While the riders dismounted and tied their ponies, the sheriff explained the trick to throw the bandits off the scent.

"Wal, why hold us?" demanded a puzzled guard. "Ain't we supposed t' ride ahead and draw the gunfire, if any?"

"I'm a-goin' to switch the sacks," returned Tex calmly, as he hunkered in the shade.

"Switch 'em agen!" The guard rubbed his bristly jaw. "One of us is crazy and it shore ain't me."

The sheriff smiled serenely. "Wal, we'll jest wait and see."

Bumping behind the two fast-stepping broncs, the buggy whirled into the midst of the tethered ponies and lounging men.

"What's cookin'?" yelled Barlow, pulling his team down. "You gents been held up already?"

"Nope," said Tex, walking to the side of the buggy. "We're a-goin' to switch the payroll."

"Figgered you were takin' too big a chance?" smiled the express agent. "Wal, I'm not sorry, f'r one. Thet dinero sure weighs heavy on my mind."

In double quick time, the boxes were transferred. The wagon creaked away, with its screen of outriders. Barlow swung his buggy around.

"Hey, hold it!" yelled Tex. "You foller the wagon in an hour."

"Like hell I do!" yelled the indignant express agent. "Drive this team with a box of sand t' the mines! I won't hit town agen 'til sundown and I got work aplenty back there."

"This buggy dogs the wagon!" The sheriff's voice was brittle.

"But thet's plumb foolishness!" expostulated Barlow. "We gotta Express shipment due and my helper quit."

"You drive t' the mines!" reiterated the sheriff.

Barlow's angry eyes flicked from the Texan's bleak features to Winters, the deputy.

"Give yuh a ten-spot t' make the run," he snapped to Winters.

The sharp-featured deputy looked eagerly at the sheriff. "Okay with you, Tex? It'll be a picnic."

"Suits me," shrugged the Texan

"Thank Gawd!" breathed Barlow. "I only agreed to make this fool trip because Heinie wouldn't trust no one else."

An hour later, Winters mounted to the buggy seat and snapped the lines. Barlow swung across the deputy's pony.

The sheriff grabbed his reins. "Dumb up when yuh hit town."

"Ain't yuh ridin'?"

"Nope. I'm tailin' the buggy."

"All yuh need is a camel and you'd have a circus parade!" With this parting shot, the express agent spurred his mount and streaked for home.

Tex finished his cigarette, leisurely ground the butt beneath his boot, then forked his buckskin and ambled westward along the wagon trail. For a while it cut across the mesquite flats. Then the terrain changed. The earth swelled up into low rolling hills, rock-pitted and scantily clothed with squat oak, with piñon in the draws. Far distant, the belching smelter smudged the blue sky. Quail twittered in the low-lying brush. Peace enveloped the gray landscape, slumbering in the sweltering heat.

As though a packet of firecrackers had been ignited, a salvo of rifle shots, faintly spluttering in the hills ahead, pricked up the ears of the drowsy buckskin. Tex snapped into quick attention. Straightening, he spurred the pony into a canter, urged it with voice and steel into a pounding gallop. Its hooves drummed upon the trail as it flew around the flanks of ridges, plunged through the shallow draws, clattered across rock-littered washes, the dust boiling in its wake.

Eyes searching ahead, Tex suddenly ripped out a terse oath. Pounding toward him came two maddened broncs, heads stretched out, tails streaming. Behind them, the buggy pumped and careened, swaying wildly from side to side and threatening every moment to overturn.

At sight of the oncoming rider, the runaways swerved and hit into a narrow canyon. They quickly tangled the thick brush and were brought to a halt, with heaving chests and wild eyes.

Tex, in full pursuit, drew abreast and eyed the buggy. Winters and the bullion box were gone.

Quickly knotting the broncs' reins around a tree trunk, he left them and spurred back to the trail. Half a mile westward he found what he sought. Sprawled in a gully beside the wagon road were the remains of Winters. The flesh puckered around two bullet holes in his chest. His brains spilled through a gaping hole, where a slug had smashed his head. The stiffening muscles of his forearm still tensed the hand that grasped his six-gun. On the road lay the box—empty.

CHAPTER 10

Lips tight pressed, Tex eyed the crumpled remains of his deputy. The story was plain—a sudden attack, quick looting of the dummy payroll and a fast getaway. Someone had tipped off the bandits that the gold had been switched to the buggy . . . and that someone was either Barlow, the express agent, or one of the three bank employees. No one else knew. Barlow and Heinemann, the sheriff ruled out. That left the two clerks—the lanky Markham and Bradley, the graying cashier.

Tex swung into leather and rode back to the canyon. He backed the broncs, now quieted, loaded Winters's remains and tied his buckskin to the buggy. Then he hit for town.

Shadows crept across Main Street when the trail-weary team halted outside the bank. The doors were closed and the premises darkened, but a lamp burned bright in Heinemann's private office. Tex threw a handful of pebbles against the window. The manager pered out, features paling as he glimpsed the buggy. Quickly he slipped out of a side door and almost ran toward the sheriff in his anxiety.

"They've got another payroll!" he exclaimed, voice strained.

"Nope, but they got Winters. Take a look at this!"

Tex led Heinemann across the plankwalk and indicated the still figure heaped on the buggy.

The banker shuddered at sight of the dead man's blood-splattered features. "I—don't understand," he jerked out. "Barlow left here with the payroll and now—" He paused in bewilderment.

In short, clipped sentences the sheriff told of the switch and Winters's killing. "Someone talked," he concluded grimly, "and Winters paid, with his life."

"But no one knew, except Barlow, outside the bank."

"Thet narrows it down t' three men," returned Tex harshly. The sheriff was in a black mood. The killing of Winters, crowding close on Kathryn's apparent duplicity, had stirred him to the depths.

"You're not questioning the trustworthiness of my staff?" challenged Heinemann haughtily.

"You bet your boots I am," rasped Tex. "Either Markham or Bradley sold us out and I'll gamble it ain't the first time."

"Bert Bradley has worked in this bank for twenty years. I'll stake my soul on his honesty."

"And Markham?"

"Markham is the son of Charles Markham, superintendent of the Concha Copper Company, a director of the bank."

"Do you happen to know if he lives on his pay?"

"Certainly."

"Then he lives high. I've seen him playin' poker in The Double Eagle f'r table stakes that would choke a steer."

"Reg Markham may be young and a little reck-

less," protested the banker, "but his honesty is un-
questioned."

"I'll question it jest as soon as I steer Winters
into the funeral parlor," snapped Tex. "This is
murder, Heinemann. That poor jasper," he nodded
at the still form on the buggy, "was killed because one of yore men either ran off at the mouth
like a damn jackass, or is an all-fired, double-
crossin' rattlesnake."

The bank manager's face reddened with suppressed anger and his eyes sparked, but he locked
his lips. The truth of the sheriff's heated words was
too apparent.

Leaving the indignant manager standing on the
plankwalk, Tex climbed back to the buggy seat and
headed the team toward the undertaker's "parlor"
—a horse barn—behind the Western Mercantile
Store.

The body disposed of, he left the ponies at the
livery and strode toward The Double Eagle. It was
midweek and few punchers were around, but Pat
O'Keefe's popular rendezvous was well filled with
townsmen, sluicing the dust of their dry throats
and relaxing around the liquor-stained card tables.

Tex stepped inside the door, peering through the
drifting haze of tobacco smoke for a glimpse of the
lanky bank clerk. He sighted Markham at a table
in company with two pallid-featured gamblers and
a grizzled cowman. Unobserved, he drifted close,
watching the play. Eyes covered by a green eye-
shade, a supple-fingered gambler flipped out the
pasteboards. Chips were heaped high before
Markham and Tex noted that he sloshed whiskey
freely into his glass from a half-filled bottle on the
table. Unnaturally bright, the clerk's eyes darted

up at the sheriff's silent form. As quickly, they were averted.

"Scared," thought the Texan. "Kinda well heeled, ain't yuh?" he inquired, nodding at the stacked chips.

"I—I've been lucky," returned the clerk quickly.

"Yore luck's done turned, mister," said Tex laconically. "Reckon I need yuh up at the courthouse."

"What do you mean? I've done nothing. You've no right to interfere with respectable citizens. Leave me alone!" jabbered Markham, stark fear dawning in his eyes.

"Start walkin'," growled Tex.

The cowman leaned back in his chair, teeth clamped on a thick cigar, and watched the by-play curiously. Eyes guarded, the gamblers silently studied their hands.

"What's your charge?" blustered the clerk. His fingers, clutching the five cards, jerked nervously, upsetting his glass. The liquor flowed around the stacked chips. Spasmodically, he clutched at the overturned glass and dropped the pasteboards on the table, face up.

"Dead man's hand." The green-shaded gambler's voice was cold and unemotional.

Markham stared wildly at the blackjacks and eights. "Why should I die? I've done nothing—"

"Let's git goin'," interjected Tex impatiently. His fingers fastened on Markham's thin shoulder and he jerked the youth to his feet.

"You can't do this!" expostulated the suspect. He writhed and struggled like a fish on a hook as the sheriff steered him inexorably toward the batwings.

Outside, Tex cut his protests short. "Save yore breath f'r the jury," he grunted. "You'll need it!"

The clerk lapsed into sullen silence and paced reluctantly beside him down the darkened street.

At the office, the sheriff nodded curtly toward a seat. He sank into the swivel chair, slowly rolled a smoke and eyed Markham silently.

"Well?" burst out the clerk. "Now you've got me here what do you want to know?"

"Whose payroll are you on, besides the bank's?"

The lanky youth jumped to his feet. "You can't insult me! My father's a director of the bank. You'll lose your job for this, you fool!"

"Set down!" said Tex stonily. "And plug your talk box. We switched the mine payroll today. Jest four hombres knew, outside of me. One of them tipped off the gang that's raisin' hell in Smoky Valley. I've tallied three and they're okay. Yo're the fourth."

Markham's jaw quivered but the sheriff held up a restraining hand. "You ain't heard it all yet. They's a dead man in the shed behind the mercantile store and it ain't Ted Barlow. Afore he died he talked—plenty. Yo're a gambler, wal, here's yore chance t' rake in the pot. Spill yore guts and I'll let you saddle yore pony and give yuh an hour's start to the border. Act dumb and you go in the jug on a murder charge. Five men was killed in that last holdup."

He slipped a match from his hatband, touched it to his cigarette and watched the clerk through narrowed eyes.

Markham perched nervously on the edge of his chair, hands interlocked, restless fingers twining and intertwining. His eyes were focused on the butt-littered floor.

Tex rose, lifted the cell keys off their peg, jingled them loudly. "Make up yore mind!" he grated.

Markham's hand jerked up, he shrank back as the sheriff approached, cleared his throat tremulously. "Will you keep your word if I talk?" he croaked.

"A hoss and an hour's start," reiterated Tex.

Markham dabbed his wet forehead with a white handkerchief. "I'll—I'll talk."

The sheriff turned away to hang up the keys. A bullet snicked through a windowpane with a crisp tinkle. Tex spun around, to see Markham fall forward and sprawl across the floor. A gun flash blossomed at a second-story window in the hotel across the street. As the sharp crack of the explosion hit the sheriff's ears a second bullet droned like a hornet past his head. He dropped to the floor, pulled his gun and snapped a shot at the bracketed lamp. The light petered out. He jumped up and leaped toward the window.

Silence draped the darkened hotel. Tex scanned the row of windows, dim in the starlight. All gaped open to admit the cool night air. Not a movement marked the hideout of the assassin.

The sheriff turned away and bent over Markham's limp body. The clerk's voice was stilled —forever. By luck or marksmanship the first bullet had taken him through the heart. Tex cursed softly beneath his breath. In another two minutes the weak-kneed accomplice of the payroll bandits would have talked plenty and the veil of mystery that shrouded the gang would have been torn aside. Markham's quick killing was proof aplenty that the gangsters had connections in town and that they would stop at nothing.

These thoughts flashed through the sheriff's mind as he straightened and hit for the door. At a run, he descended the courthouse steps and crossed the street.

The hands of the old Ward clock above the hotel desk indicated it was past eleven. Sam Tucker, the wizened clerk, snored in his chair, steel spectacles askew on his bulbous nose. The lobby was peopled by shadows cast by a kerosene lamp suspended from the center of the ceiling.

Tex shook Sam into bemused wakefulness. "Hear them gunshots?" he demanded, nose wrinkling at the reek of liquor.

Sam shook his bald head. "Nope," he rumbled, blinking rheumy eyes, "I was snatching a mite of shuteye." He blinked after Tex's fast-moving form as the sheriff bounded up the stairway, then fumbled at the neck of a square gin bottle that was beneath his chair.

A wide corridor ran the length of the second floor, bedrooms opening off on either side. At each end of the corridor and at the head of the stairway, oil lamps, turned low, gave feeble light.

Tex's brief sight of the gun flashes led him to believe that the shots were fired from a room in the center of the building. He dashed around the angle of the corridor and ran full tilt into a group of hastily garbed men in unbuttoned shirts and dragging pants, excitedly discussing the gunplay. One pair of bony feet protruded from beneath an ankle-length nightshirt.

Crowding like a flock of clucking hens, they deluged the sheriff with loud-voiced explanations.

Wearily Tex held up his hand. "Take it easy, gents!" he begged. Quickly he sized up the circle, nodded at a poker-faced cowman. "You tell it, mister!"

"Ain't much t' tell," drawled the cowman. "Some gink want haywire with a saddle gun in thet room." He nodded toward an open door. "I grabbed my iron and moseyed out, cautious like, when a gent streaks by like a bat outer hell, skedaddles down the hallway and vamooses pronto."

"Did you git a look at his face?" asked Tex eagerly.

The cowman shook his head. "Nope, the light ain't too good and thet hombre moved faster'n a tin-canned dawg."

Tex walked to the end of the corridor, the motley group of awakened sleepers straggling in his wake. A door provided egress to an open stairway, which led to the ground. It bore the legend, "Use in case of fire only."

Retracing his steps, the sheriff entered the room from which the shots were fired. The stench of burned powder still fouled the air. A quick glance revealed that the bed was made up and the window open wide. Tex touched a match to a lamp on the washstand, dropped low and examined the dusty carpet. Two empty shells lay on the floor beneath the window.

"Sharp's 50-70," muttered Tex, as he slipped them into a pants pocket. "Don't help none, most every waddy totes thet caliber saddle gun."

Through the window frame he glanced across

the street, down into his office. He fancied he could see the outline of Markham's figure stretched across the floor.

"Thet hairpin was a durned fancy shot," he mused. He pushed through the curious men clustered at the door and hustled downstairs to the lobby.

"Who booked 215?" he barked.

The old clerk rose unsteadily, adjusted his glasses and peered at the blotted register. Then he turned and squinted at the key board.

"No one," he droned. "Look at the key, settin' up there!"

Tex eyed the key. It was made for a common mortise lock. Then he rounded the showcase that served as a counter and examined other keys that dangled from their hooks.

"I'll gamble every one of them keys ull open every door in the joint?" he commented.

"You said it!" chuckled Sam. "It's mighty convenient, Sheriff." He slid open a drawer. "Lookee! We got lotsa extras. Ain't many gents turns their keys in."

"Yo're sure a helpful cuss," grunted Tex in disgust.

A bulky figure loomed out of the gloom as he stepped into the street.

"From whence come wars and fighting?" boomed the Preacher's deep voice.

"Some bushwhacker jest plugged a jasper in my office. Got him from a hotel window."

"Oh that men would obey the Lord's command —love one another," sighed Paul, as he swing up the courthouse steps beside the sheriff. "Who was the victim of the miserable gunman?"

"Clerk from the bank. He's been crossin' us, tipped off the gold shipments. Was jest spillin' his guts when he was rubbed out."

"Did he give—names?"

Tex's perception, keyed to a high pitch by the tragic end of the would-be informant, detected a note of excitement, of suppressed eagerness, in the Preacher's deep tones. He glanced curiously at the bearded face by his side, but it told him nothing.

"Nope!" he returned shortly.

"Is Markham badly hit?"

"He's dead!"

"The wages of sin is death." Fervently the Preacher intoned the Biblical quotation, then stopped, midway up the steps. "I was about to retire to rest when those shots disturbed the peacefulness of the night. I will seek my bed. He who lives by the sword shall die by the sword. Adios!"

A question in his eyes, Tex watched the Preacher's big figure until it melted into the night. "Mighty curious," he mused. "The Preacher's a crack shot. Whenever there's trouble he jest naturally slides into the picture. And how in hell did he know it was Markham who was rubbed out?"

CHAPTER 11

Dan Cummings, the desert-dried old sheriff, was as hard to kill as the fiery-eyed bald eagle to which he bore such a striking resemblance. He lay abed in his home, a frame shack on the edge of town, shadowed by fluffing cottonwoods.

It was here that Tex found him the morning after Markham's murder, in response to an imperious summons.

Mrs. Cummings, a motherly matron who might have been politely described as "pleasingly plump," in crisp starched gingham, opened the door in answer to his knock.

"How's Dan?" inquired the Texan.

"Cross as a snapping turtle, but what man isn't when he's tied to his bed," sighed the good lady. "But he's mending, thank the Lord!"

Tex followed her into a cheerful, white-curtained bedroom where the sheriff was propped up with pillows in an ornate brass bedstead; the bedclothes were littered with papers and periodicals.

As unblinking as ever, his bleak eyes focused on his deputy's lean features.

"Hear you been raisin' hell with the payroll snatchers?"

"I come mighty close t' gettin' the deadwood on 'em last night," returned Tex complacently. He settled into a chair beside the bed, stretched his long legs and shook out the makin's.

"But yuh didn't!"

"Nope, some sidewinder plugged the windy—thet slab-sided bank clerk Markham."

Cummings nodded impatiently. "Preacher tole me 'smorning."

"I don't savvy this Preacher," said Tex slowly. "Gun speed and bible punchin' don't mix."

"What yuh got agenst him?" demanded Cummings irately.

"Nothin', except a hunch."

"Wal, ferget it. Preacher Paul's a heap good hombre. He eased you out of a tight, didn't he?"

"Looks like that long beard been runnin' off at the mouth aplenty." Tex's voice was taut.

"Looks like he ain't the only bellerin' calf around here," returned the old sheriff dryly. His manner changed. "Keep thet gun oiled, Tex. I figger they're liable t' drop you next. When yuh stir up a hornets' nest they'll likely sting. You done hoswiggled them out of a stock of dinero and they ain't too sure Markham didn't squawk."

"Who in hell are 'they'?" demanded the Texan irritably.

"The orneriest bunch of snake-blooded killers thet ever cursed Concha County. They wiped Winters out like he was a hound dawg, they killed half a dozen good men afore him, and they jest rubbed out Markham. Mebbe they got you measured for a box."

"Ef you ain't a cheerful old cuss!" exclaimed the Texan, with a twisted grin. "What's my play—light a shuck, like a tin-canned pup?"

"Nope." The old sheriff's voice was sober. "Jest

watch yore step an' swear in a coupla more good deputies. These varmints are plumb pison. Goshamighty, wisht I could straddle a pony!"

➤ "Poor old Dan's got the heebie-jeebies," Tex told the buckskin, as he jogged easily back to the courthouse. "Them highbinders got him jiggeroed. He jest snoozes in thet fancy bed and gits the most orful nightmares. Ef I'd told him about the O'Keefe gal I gamble he'd have hit the roof."

Two days later a wiry, dark-featured man eased quietly through the batwings of The Double Eagle. As the doors swung back behind him, he paused to allow his eyes to focus after the sun-glare outside. Sharp and quick-moving, they darted around, not fearfully but with an eternal watchfulness that was emphasized by the twin guns thonged down at his sides.

It was early afternoon, and the saloon was deserted save for Kathryn O'Keefe, busying herself behind the bar.

The girl eyed the stranger curiously as he moved toward her over the sawdust with short springy steps. The thought leaped into her mind of a cat about to spring, or, better a panther—silent and dangerous. She knew every puncher within fifty miles by sight, but this man was a newcomer. Her eyes ran over his stubbled jaw and lined, homely features. His dark pants were stuffed carelessly into cowman's boots. He wore a flannel shirt and loose-hanging vest. A well-worn cartridge belt sagged from his lean hips. From his twin holsters the walnut butts of his guns gleamed with the smooth polish of long use. Jet black hair straggled from beneath a shabby Stetson, which was circled by a dried rattle-snake's skin.

"A touch o'bourbon, ma'am!" His voice as he slid up to the bar was mild, almost apologetic.

She set out bottle and glass. The stranger tossed a dollar on the boards and poured himself a scant two fingers. He sipped it slowly, his gaze focused on her.

Kathryn shrank back as she met his scrutiny, for the newcomer's eyes pierced like twin rapiers, hard as lava knobs, merciless as a rattlesnake's.

"Jasper by name of Tex in town?" he inquired gently.

She nodded mutely, possessed by a nameless dread.

The stranger's lips twisted in the ghost of a satisfied smile. He jerked a tobacco sack out of a pocket of his sagging vest.

"Seen him around lately?"

"He's our sheriff."

"Kind of interferin' cuss?" The newcomer deftly rolled a smoke and twisted the end.

"He does his duty," she retorted hotly. "What do you want with him?"

"I come t' kill him." So matter-of-factly and unemotionally were the words spoken that the bewildered girl could only stare, scarce believing the evidence of her ears.

"You've come to—what?" she gulped.

"Kill him."

"Why—what has he ever done to you?"

"Nothin'."

Kathryn backed along the bar. The man was not drunk, he must be crazy.

A slow smile curved the stranger's thin lips as he

observed her agitation.

"That's my business," he said simply. "Gun-nie!"

"You'd kill a man—for pay!" Cold contempt smothered Kathryn's fear. She stared at the shabby figure in amazement.

"You said it, lady," he returned indifferently. "Gimme a stinker. will yuh!"

Bending quickly, she snatched the double-bar-reled ten-gauge shotgun from beneath the bar and backed, covering him fearfully.

"You move and I'll give you both barrels!" she warned, voice shrill with emotion. "Don't take a step, now! I'm going to warn him."

"Suits me, lady," he returned indifferently, trickling a little more whiskey into the glass. "Tell him I'll be on the street in ten minutes. Say, this joint carries a dandy brand of bourbon!"

Breathless, with glowing cheeks, Kathryn stood by the spur-scratched desk in the sheriff's office and gasped out her story of the cold-eyed killer.

Tex listened in amused silence. When she paused to catch her breath, he pushed back the squeaky swivel chair and reached for his gun-belt.

"What are you going to do?" she demanded.

"Go git this hairpin."

"Don't, Tex!" implored the girl. Her small fingers fastened on his hard-muscled forearm. "He's a paid killer. Your death would be just another job. Get some deputies. Surround the saloon!"

"And my name would be mud in Hanging Wells," he answered dryly. "Ain't nothin' t' git scared of, ma'am. I reckon he's some locoed tinhorn, goin' off half-cocked."

Kathryn shuddered. "He's a paid gunman. They hired him to kill you."

"Who hired him—yore pals?"

She paled, white teeth biting into her lower lip. "Is that—your thanks?" Her voice was subdued. Dully, she turned away and walked slowly toward the door. Perplexity mirrored in his eyes, the Texan watched her lithe form. As she disappeared into the corridor, he took an impetuous step forward, then he shrugged his shoulders, pulled out his gun, spun the cylinder and checked the loads.

Nothing disturbed the serenity of Main Street's mid-afternoon when the sheriff thudded hollowly down the courthouse steps. Wagons and buckboards creaked and rattled through lazily drifting dust. Ponies drowsed at the hitch rails. Along the shaded plankwalks drifted housewives, punchers and Mexicans, shopping, chatting or just lounging. A pack of mongrels tore at a piece of offal outside the butcher's shop, a yelling Mexican youth hazed a bearded billy goat, a drummer snored peacefully under the faded hotel awning.

At the entrance to the hotel, a vivid patch of crimson pulled the Texan's questing eyes. He raised his right hand mechanically at Diane Cresswell's clear-voiced greeting and continued his search for sight of the gunman.

A medium-sized man in dark pants, the brim of his battered Stetson turned down to shade his eyes, stepped out of The Double Eagle, slipped under the hitch rail and walked out into the street. Tex's searching eyes took in the twin guns in laced down holsters. At the distance the stranger's features were a dark blur.

The Texan stepped off the plankwalk onto the street, pock-marked by countless hooves. Slowly, obliquely across the wide thoroughfare, the two men approached each other, their boots stirring up tiny streamers of dust, arms stiff at their sides.

By some mysterious means, word swept along the plankwalks that a gunfight was brewing. In a trice, it seemed, the hitch rails were bare of ponies and the lumbering wagons and jolting buckboards pulled off into alleyways. The plankwalks cleared as if by magic. Women huddled in store entrances, heads poked from doorways, the windows of the hotel were suddenly white with eager faces.

Save for the two figures, their elongated shadows slanting sideways, slowly and inexorably closing in, the street was deserted.

A woman's shriek cut through the brooding quiet. With a gleeful yell, a four-year-old in cut-down overalls darted out into the sun-swept street, directly between the two silent, shuffling figures. Long dress trailing and sun-bonnet awry, a woman dashed out, gathered the child in her arms and skittered for shelter.

The two men were not fifty paces distant now. Never hesitating, they continued to advance—forty, thirty paces. Tex stopped, slightly bent, his hand, half closed, caressing the butt of the gun in his swiveled open-toed holster. The dust slowly settled around his feet as the stranger dropped into a crouch and stood, still as a statue, hands poised above his guns.

"You want me?" The sheriff's voice carried to a hundred straining ears.

"I reckon I do." Low-voiced, the gunman's reply scarce reached the Texan.

"What's the trouble?"

"Jest a matter of business."

"Then git me!" As he snapped out the challenge, Tex's hand closed on the gun butt. The swiveled holster jerked out and lanced red. Tex was fast, but even as he squeezed the trigger he knew the stranger was faster.

The dark-featured man's right hand flicked down and his gun flashed out and up in one smooth, split-second motion. But as it arched through the air, faster than a snake strikes, a trembling needle of dancing light shot from the plankwalk. A spot of dazzling radiance flickered over his dark face and fastened on his eyes.

His gun blared a split second ahead of the sheriff's. Tex heard the drone of the slug. Then he was aware of nothing save the crouching form ahead, at which his jumping gun sprayed hot lead.

The lash of gunfire mingled and blended as forty-fives roared and scarlet flashes bit through the powder haze. Tortured by the blinding spot of darting light, the stranger shook his head savagely, sidestepped—in vain. Then, of a sudden, he jerked erect, his gun arm dropped limp and the smoking iron plunked into the dust. Blood gushed from his slackened mouth. He swayed uncertainly, crashed down. For a moment or two his limbs jerked spasmodically, then he lay still, very still.

Gripping the butt of the gun in his up-tilted holster, the Texan moved close. He hooked his boot under the sprawled figure and eased it over. The staring eyes of the stranger gazed unseeingly into the blue sky. Somberly Tex turned away, as excited punchers and townsfolk cascaded into the street.

Ignoring the shouted congratulations and backslapping of the men who pressed around, Tex headed for The Double Eagle. Savagely booting back the swinging doors, he pushed inside.

Kathryn, alone, was standing by the window.

"You got a hand mirror?" he jerked out.

"What if I have?" Her voice was icy.

"Some interferin' female blinded that hombre."

"And saved your life."

"I don't crave thet brand of help," he replied stonily.

"Well, Tex Tevis, if it's any news, I wouldn't lift a hand to save your worthless hide if you were attacked by twenty gunmen."

He searched her flushed features, then, with a grunt, turned and strode away.

Shouldering past knots of voluble men clustered on the plankwalk, Tex headed for his office, groping in his mind for a solution to the mystery of the flashing mirror. Someone had blinded the gunman, otherwise he had a grim foreboding that it would have been his lifeless remains they would have packed into the barn behind the mercantile store. His thoughts flew to Diana Cresswell. She was standing at the hotel entrance. In his grim concentration on the business at hand he had lost sight of her. Her quick wit had once opened the door of his cell. Had she saved him from a hired killer?

CHAPTER 12

Shoulders stooped from long bending over plow and harrow, leathery faces seamed from a lifetime's battle with the elements, gnarled hands toughened from toil, a bunch of farmers, "fool hoemen" the punchers labeled them, clumped awkwardly up the courthouse steps.

Close-lipped and morose, they crowded into the sheriff's office.

Aroused from his noon siesta, Tex hastily removed his feet from the desk top and thrust the brim of his Stetson back from the tip of his nose. Swinging around, he turned questioning eyes on the visitors, noted their clumsy boots, soil-stained overalls, faded hickory shirts. More, he observed the anger reflected on the encircling faces.

"Wal, gents," he inquired affably, "what's eatin' yuh?"

Their gaze turned to a stalwart fellow with steady eyes and neatly trimmed beard, evidently the leader.

"We have come for justice." His deep, sonorous tones reminded the sheriff of Preacher Paul.

"You shore hit the right spot. Some varmint run off yore hosses?"

The bearded man gestured impatiently. "We at-

107

tend to such matters. This is a far greater calamity.
One Cresswell, a cowman, burned our homes, ran
off our cows, drove us by force of arms from land
that was legally ours."

"What's yore name?" asked Tex, curiously
aroused by the bearded nester's precise speech.

"Aaron Falk."

"Mormon?"

The other nodded.

"These gents Mormons, too?"

"No, they come from many states to this great
western land to build homes and raise families. I
led the wagon train."

"So Cresswell hazed yuh out of Smoky Valley,"
pondered the Texan. "Wal, what are yuh goin' t'
do about it?"

"What can we do?" The Mormon raised his
arms high, as though to appeal to heaven. "We are
peaceful men, we demand protection and redress."

"Anyone killed in the ruckus?"

"No one, the Lord be thanked."

"Then I can't do a danged thing t' help yuh!"

A growl rumbled deep in the throats of the assembled nesters.

"Ain't you the sheriff?" rasped a truculent
hoeman, eyes flashing beneath black brows.

"Shore," agreed Tex equably. "But you gents
don't savvy the cow country. The cowmen drove
out the Apaches and grabbed every waterhole, every square yard of graze. They was lords of creation. You jaspers roll in, fence off the waterholes,
plow up the land, string barbed wire and the cowmen go on the prod. They fought t' win this range
and they ain't backward in fightin' t' hold it. This

town lives off'n cow money. I couldn't raise a posse t' help yuh ef I offered twenty dollars a day and found."

"But the land is ours," pointed out Aaron Falk patiently. "We filed at the land office and paid our fees. The law says—"

Tex checked the Mormon with upraised hand, his lips curved sardonically. "They's only one law in the West, mister, gun law, and Judge Colt rods it." He sobered at sight of the bewilderment in the Mormon's calm eyes. "I know how you feel. Monte Moreland, foreman of the Box-C, run me off my homestead and killed my brother. I aim t' even that score, but the law book won't help any."

"So we got t' fight?" challenged the belligerent nester.

At Tex's curt nod, he elbowed to the Mormon's side. "Ain't that what I claimed, give 'em slug f'r slug!"

Falk shook his graying head. "He who lives by the sword shall die by the sword."

"He shore speaks the Preacher's jargon," thought Tex. Aloud he said, "Yuh gotta stand on yore own feet out here, bud."

Eyes flashing, the black-browed nester addressed his fellows, "Are we goin' t' let this Cresswell coyote chase us out like a bunch of jack-rabbits? Aaron here kin set out on the flats and starve 'til his belly flattens agenst his backbone, but I'm a-goin' back ef you jaspers ull side me. I got a buffalo gun thet'll out-range them hawglegs."

A storm of debate arose, in which the sheriff was forgotten. Arms folded, the Mormon stood apart, his counsels of prudence ignored by the sorely tried hoemen.

At length, behind Mike Curman, the black-browed nester, they streamed down the courthouse steps, defiance in their patient eyes.

At sunup, the sheriff rode out upon an arid flat south of town, where the big-wheeled wagons, with bulging hooped tops, grayed with desert dust, were set in a wide circle.

Within the circle, women bustled around a dozen campfires. Shouting boys were hazing horses and mules in from the brush, others were adjusting neck yokes, hefting wagon tongues and hooking up traces.

Screened by a mesquite clump, Tex watched. The crack of a whip snapped through the sharp morning air as a wagon pulled out of the circle behind a team of plodding mules. Others followed, until nine wagons crawled like great centipedes through the sparse brush, heading westward into the purple haze that was Smoky Valley. Three remained.

A tight smile creased the Texan's lean features. "I been hopin' f'r a showdown," he informed the restless buckskin, "and it looks like it's come. The Box-C can't rod this range forever."

Events moved faster in Smoky Valley than Tex had even dared to hope. Busy with routine duties, he quickly forgot the nesters' wagons, snaking into the valley. Before the day died, however, a wild-eyed youth spurred out of the scarlet sunset and plunged into the sheriff's office.

"Hell's a-poppin' mister!" he gasped. "Them

measly cowhands threw down on us while we was spread out, pullin' through a canyon. They got Laff Lewis, Tod Sneath, and Bill Hummock. Tod's team bolted, wheel rolled over Tod and—''

"Take it easy, son, and set down," counseled Tex kindly. He pushed the quivering lad into a chair.

"Yore pards makin' a stand, or headin' back?"

"Hittin' for town, I reckon."

"How's the wimmen and kids?"

"Goshdarn ef I know," confessed the youth, brushing the long hair back from his forehead. "Mike said t' ride like old Harry f' the sheriff, so I hightailed."

"Can't do much 'til sunup," mused Tex. He smiled at the trail-weary messenger. "I gamble yo're hungry enough t' eat a saddle blanket."

"Never give a thought to eatin', mister, but now yuh mention it, I reckon my belt is kinda slack."

"Any dinero?"

With a wry grin, the boy turned out the pockets of his overalls.

Tex tossed him a dollar. "Drop into the Chinaman's and eat. Then stick around yore old stampin' ground; the Mormon's still in camp. See yuh later."

Next morning, the remnants of the wagon trail limped in—five wagons, packed with sorrowing women and squawling children.

The black-browed nester, Mike Curman, who had led them, rode up to Tex with bitter eyes.

"Three men dead and four wounded," he gritted, "and we got the law on our side! D'ye aim t' do anything about it, Mister Law Man, or has them Box-C bustards got yuh buffaloed?"

"Gather up yore men f'r a powwow," directed the sheriff curtly.

Axles creaking, the surviving wagons pulled into a circle and silent men unhitched the teams. Hopelessness was mirrored in their dull eyes and drooping shoulders. For days, weeks, they had inched across the plains, forded rivers, spanned mountains, to reach the Promised Land. Now at journey's end, they were ruthlessly attacked, their possessions looted, their wagons destroyed, because they dared attempt to settle on land which was legally theirs. Against hard-riding, quick-shooting punchers these men had no more chance than sheep harried by wolves. They were peaceful farmers, men with families in their wagons and plows lashed to the tailboards.

Somberly they gathered around the tall sheriff with ill-veiled hostility; for he represented the law, and the law had failed them.

"So the Box-C boys jumped yuh," commented Tex, dark eyes probing their weathered faces. "Kin yuh swear t' any of the hairpins thet flung lead?"

"I lamped one!" volunteered Curman eagerly. "A hook-nosed jasper, black as an Injun, rode a hoss with white shoes."

"Yep, he shot Laff Lewis," broke in another. "Yelled like an Apache when Laff tumbled out of the wagon seat."

"Thet's Monte Moreland, the Box-C foreman." Tex's voice was hard. "I'll go git him, ef you boys ull help me. I want six men; can't raise a posse in town."

"Won't they plug us? I got a family," ventured a stocky nester.

"Yep, there's mebbe twenty-thirty waddies at the Box-C home ranch," agreed the sheriff. "They might fill yuh full of holes, but I'll deputize you boys. I reckon the Colonel ull think twice afore he trades lead with a sheriff's posse."

"Pick yore men, Sheriff?" cut in Curman grimly. "And count me in. Guess there ain't a man here who won't take a chance t' put thet murderin' Apache where he belongs."

Tex quickly singled out five of the younger men. "Raise yore right hands," he directed.

Mounted on an assortment of flop-eared mules and blocky ponies, the ungainly appearance of the nester posse caused Tex to smother a smile hastily. They formed a striking contrast to the typical narrow-hipped, devil-may-care puncher, swaying easily in the saddle of a frisky cow pony. These hoemen were thick-set, solemn-featured men in homespun and overalls. Their thick-soled boots were spurless and they sat heavily in the saddle. But their tanned features were stamped with stubborn determination and every man toted a shotgun, a Spencer or a Henry.

At the head of his uncouth cavalcade, the sheriff heeled his pony and dipped down into the valley.

Colonel Cresswell's sprawling homespread lay fifteen miles northwest of the county seat. Tex held the buckskin down to a jog-trot, the nesters, sweating and sliding in the saddle, bumping in his rear. He headed down the center of the valley, across endless rolling swales, lush cow country hock deep in grama and specked with bunches of Box-C steers.

To the west of the great shallow bowl that was

Cresswell's domain slumbered the gaunt Smokies, their rugged silhouettes quivering through the shimmering heat waves. Southward, the Concha Copper Company's smelter begrimed the sky. Ahead lay an ocean of grass, flooding into purple infinity.

Tex, in the lead, topped a low rise and drew rein. The nesters bumped up beside him and eyed the Box-C spread, not a quarter-mile ahead. Centering it was the ranch house, long, low and massive, built of rock-and-adobe, a rugged home that reflected the character of the granite-faced Colonel. Behind it were grouped the bunkhouse, blacksmith shop, barns and corrals. A windmill circled lazily, its metal blades flashing in the sun.

With inward misgiving, Tex tallied two dozen ponies drifting around the horse corral. The shrill yippees of two punchers topping broncs floated through the still air. Other men moved among the outbuildings.

The Texan swung around in the saddle and surveyed his possemen. "Them jasper's are liable t' dish out a dose of lead," he drawled; "ef any of you don't stomach the odds now's the time t' beat it."

The nesters met his gaze in solid silence.

He grinned. "You got sand, boys! Now, lissen, keep them itchy trigger fingers under control. Ef there's a fracas, they'll fill us so full of holes we won't float in brine. Foller my lead." With this admonition, he spurred the buckskin and dropped down toward the ranch.

In a disordered group, the posse drew rein and milled around in front of the ranch house. Tex swung out of leather, ground-hitched his pony and clinked up to the door.

It was flung open in response to his knock and the Colonel's burly form stood framed in the entrance.

Bedded in the cold mask of his features, his hard blue eyes ran over the bunched nesters and then bored into the sheriff.

"Wal?" he ejaculated harshly.

"I rode over to serve a murder warrant," returned Tex coolly. "Thet's a legally deputized posse. Monte Moreland, and a bunch of yore boys, plugged three nesters."

The heavy-jawed cowman snorted. "Mebbe thet'll teach the sidewinders not t' chowse around Box-C range."

"They filed lawful. What right you got t' hold the range, Colonel?"

Cresswell slapped the gun holstered at his side. "King Colt, mister."

A sudden restlessness among the posse snapped Tex's head around. Around each end of the ranch house rode a column of punchers. Every saddle boot held a rifle, every gun-belt a forty-five, and the cool, competent Box-C waddies looked capable of using them to good effect.

The posse bunched tight, flustered and awkward, while the punchers ringed them as though they were herding a knot of perturbed, angry steers.

Monte Moreland pulled away and cantered up to the house.

"Wal, ef it ain't our hoeman sheriff with a bunch of his pals," he yelled derisively. "Guess they'll make good buzzard bait." He slid out of leather and stepped jauntily up to the two men. His defiant eyes challenged the Texan. "Wal, ef yo're hankerin' for trouble, mister, we kin dish out a bellyful."

"I come f'r you—charge of murder," said Tex softly.

The foreman guffawed. "Wal, ef thet don't beat all creation!" He jerked a contemptuous thumb toward the tight-bunched possemen. "We got yore nesters herded and hog-tied and you got the gall t' blow about makin' an arrest. Button yore lip!" He turned his back to the sheriff and addressed the heavy-jawed cowman. "Want we should herd them mavericks into the corral, Colonel?"

"Hold it!" barked Tex. His holster jerked up and the muzzle of his swiveled gun pressed against Cresswell's belly, bulging over a broad leather belt. "Start somethin' and I'll scatter yore guts. You ain't buckin' nesters, Moreland; thet's a legally sworn posse. Ef you men want action, by Gawd, you'll git it!"

Not a muscle moved in the cowman's rock-hewn face as he eyed the sheriff's tense features.

"You fool," he gritted, "my boys kin wipe out them nesters faster'n I could wipe my nose."

"You'd never wipe nothin'," mocked the Texan. "I'd git you first."

"I shoulda let you hang, you mangy coyote!"

"Biggest mistake yuh ever made," grinned Tex. He pressed closer. "Make up yore mind, pronto. Does Moreland go back with me?"

CHAPTER 13

"Kin I talk with the Colonel?" There was com-
promise in Moreland's tone, as though he guessed
that the sheriff had an ace in the hole and he lacked
iron to raise the ante.

Beyond the tensed group the bunch of nester
possemen packed stirrup to stirrup, shotguns and
carbines tight gripped in horny hands. Ringing
them, the bleak-eyed Box-C punchers sat stiff in
their saddles, poised for action, ready to spill flame
and thunder at a gesture from their boss. Every eye
was riveted upon the sheriff's tilted holster, hard
pressed against Cresswell's belly. Every mind
framed an unasked question. "Would the Colonel
call the tight-lipped Texan's hand and chance a
slug in his guts?"

"Go ahead!" growled Tex. "And make it snappy."

"Reckon I'll ride in," said the foreman, speaking
over the sheriff's shoulder. "No sense in startin' a
fracas. Them nesters pack shotguns."

Closely watching the Colonel's features, Tex saw
understanding flow into his eyes. Moreland, out of
the sheriff's range of vision, had made some
gesture, conveyed something beyond the words.
Tex felt Cresswell's stomach muscles relax.

"Suits me, Monte," he replied indifferently. "I'll
be seein' yuh."

"I'll take yore gun, Moreland," cut in Tex.

The foreman dabbed for his iron, but the sheriff's brittle voice stopped his arm. "Hold it! I said I'd take yore gun." His own weapon still menaced the Colonel.

Moreland shrugged his shoulders and pivoted. Tex slipped the plated forty-five from his holster.

"Kinda spooky, ain't yuh?" sneered the foreman.

"I've seen the road agent's spin afore," snapped Tex.

"I'll gamble yuh have." Moreland's voice was derisive.

Tex stuck the gun beneath his waistband and stepped behind the foreman. "Git goin'," he growled.

With dour faces, the ringing Box-C punchers watched as their foreman moved toward his pony under the threat of the sheriff's gun.

"Call yore wolves off," the sheriff gritted in his ear. "One shot and I plug yuh—it'll shore be a pleasure!"

"Hold yore hosses, boys!" yelled Moreland. "The hand ain't played yet. I'm goin' willing."

Cold sweat trickled down the Texan's spine as he jogged beside the Box-C foreman toward the posse. Never before had the range wolves of the mighty Box-C been corraled in their den and the biggest lobo of them all taken prisoner. They knew that the story of the sheriff's capture would be discussed in every saloon throughout Concha County. Their prestige had received a blow from which it would never recover. It was a bitter pill to be compelled to swallow . . . and there was yet time to spit it out.

Understanding this, Tex rode as gingerly as

though across a sagging quicksand. Every lean puncher face was darkened with chagrin. No more than a spark was needed to explode the anger that raged behind their bleak features—and he and his six nester possemen would go down beneath a hail of snarling lead.

Moreland heeled his mount into a canter. Tailing him close, Tex signaled to the posse. The nesters wheeled and dropped in behind. Relief surged through the sheriff's taut frame when he snatched a quick glance over his shoulder and saw the Box-C riders reluctantly withdrawing behind the ranch house.

The possemen's thick-legged ponies and bony mules could not hold the swinging pace of the foreman's fast pony. Quickly, they straggled, strung out into a long, laboring line.

"Pull down, Moreland!" yelled the sheriff. "This ain't a stampede."

The other checked his mount, swung around in the saddle and scornfully eyed the nesters, trailing far behind. "Figger I'll vamoose?" he sneered.

"Try and outride a bullet," invited Tex. Inwardly, the sheriff puzzled over the unspoken message that had passed between Moreland and the Colonel. Why had Cresswell agreed so casually to his foreman's offer to surrender? The pair had cooked up something. Warily, he eyed every clump of chaparral, every draw, suspecting an ambush. But nothing broke the monotony of their steady jogtrot up the sun-soaked valley.

Mike Curman spurred abreast of Tex and the prisoner, riding in the lead, as the tin roofs of shacks on the outskirts of town glittered far ahead in the slanting sun.

"How d'ye figger t' handle this gordurned Apache?" He jerked his head toward Moreland's gray-shirted figure.

"Commit him on a murder charge," replied the sheriff, with a sharp glance at the nester's hard face.

Curman frowned, resentment in his flashing eyes. "We don't see it thet way," he replied uneasily. "His hands are wet with the blood of three good men. There's widows and orphans around our wagons. The boys figger on a necktie party."

"Then they better change their notions mighty quick," replied the sheriff grimly. "This is a posse, not a mob." He jerked his pony to a sliding stop and waved down the prisoner. Wheeling, he faced the nesters, pounding in his wake. They grouped, smoldering eyes riveted on the dark features of the Box-C foreman.

"I hear you fellers got a certain notion," snapped Tex.

"Wal, ferget it! This hairpin should hang, after a fair trail. But nix on lynch law. Plug him and the county ull string up every jasper in this posse—guilty or not guilty. I reckon you got enough widders already in yore outfit."

With that, he swung his pony around and pulled beside the prisoner. "Shake it up!" he growled. Roweling their mounts, the pair plunged ahead, while the laboring possemen dropped further and further behind.

With Moreland lodged in a cell and the unruly posse plugging home somewhere out in the dusty valley, Tex relaxed with a satisfied sigh into the comfortable swivel chair. He loosened his belt, swung his long legs onto the desk and fished for the makin's. The respite was short-lived.

Spur-chains jingled in the corridor and Colonel Cresswell strode in. At his heels trotted Mortimer Mendham, a stubby little attorney with an officious manner.

Mendham clutched a sheet of paper in his pudgy hand.

"Order for the release of Monte Moreland," he announced, "signed by Judge Graham. Bail set at five hundred dollars, which Colonel Cresswell has furnished."

Tex looked over the order perfunctorily. He should have guessed, he told himself wryly, that Cresswell and his foreman had this figured out. By the time the Circuit Judge held his next session in Hanging Wells the nesters would have scattered and the case would collapse for lack of evidence. Moreland's penalty for the wholesale killing would be—he glanced at his watch—twenty minutes in a cell.

"Git a move on!" rasped Cresswell, pacing the room.

Without a word, Tex lifted the jail keys off a peg.

Ten minutes later, he watched the two Box-C bosses mount their ponies and hit homeward.

He thought of the sad-faced women in the wagons that had rolled forlornly out of the valley, of the fatherless children gazing wide-eyed from beneath the weathered canvas, of the stubborn stony-featured nesters, facing lead to bring a killer to justice. Wondered what those much-tried men would think—and do—if they passed the Colonel and his twenty-minute prisoner on the trail.

"And folks act surprised when there's a lynchin'

once in a while," he ejaculated, aiming a disgusted kick at the nearest chair.

Before noon the following day he had another visitor, shapely Diana Cresswell, cool and competent as ever, in neat riding skirt and cream shirtwaist, a peal-gray Stetson nestling on the hair that billowed around her head like a halo of pale gold.

"I thought you were a friend of mine, Tex," she challenged in her clear voice, flinging herself into a chair and smiling at his sober features.

"Yeah!" he replied guardedly, thoughts on the episode of the previous day.

"Was it nice to make the Box-C the laughing stock of the entire county?" she pouted. "And why threaten Dad?" He helped you when you needed help badly—or perhaps you have forgotten?"

The Texan bit his lip. This blue-eyed girl, with her big innocent eyes, could make a man feel lower than a rattlesnake.

"I swore t' rod the law," he countered gruffly, "and Monte's boys wiped out three nesters."

Diana lifted her slim shoulders with an eloquent gesture.

"Nesters! They're a greater pest than sheepherders. They rustle beef, fence waterholes, ruin the grass. What right have they to steal our range?"

"Homestead law," replied Tex laconically.

Wide-eyed and appealing, she leaned forward; her gloved hand touched his knee. "You're a cowman, Tex. Why help these miserable nesters? We need men like you on the range. I do so want you and Dad to be friends."

"Yore crew drove me off the range," retorted the sheriff harshly.

Diana sighed. "Let bygones be bygones. Listen, Tex! We have a ranch at Bitter River. It's beautiful country, with hills and trees and the prettiest valleys. Dad needs a man he can trust to handle it. We have trouble with renegades from across the border. I know I can persuade him to make you foreman. I spend quite a lot of time at Bitter River myself." Her voice softened. "Won't you consider it?"

He thrilled to the subtle flattery in her voice, felt the magnetism of her lithe young body—nodded.

"Wonderful!" She jumped to her feet. "Now you can buy me a lunch at the hotel," she announced gaily.

Not unmindful of the envious glances directed toward him by drummers and townsmen sitting around the hotel lobby, Tex followed the Colonel's daughter into the restaurant. It was not yet noon and there were few diners.

Diana led the way to a side table, set in a nook, by a rear window. Outwardly self-possessed, the Texan was a seething vortex of emotion within. The beauty of his companion, the obvious flattery in her eyes and manner, her suggestion of intimacy in choosing a secluded table, gave rise to thoughts that stirred him to the depths. As foreman of a Box-C ranch he would have power and prestige. Colonel Cresswell was no youngster. Some day the man who wed Diana would fall heir to a vast cattle kingdom. Why not Tex Tevis?

Against these roseate dreams battled the stark memory of a blazing ranch house, the still form of his bullet-ridden brother, the wanton killing of inoffensive nesters, the wailing of orphaned children.

Frowning, he studied the penciled menu, while

Diana fussed with a comb and hand mirror.

"Your order, please!" Tex started as if shot, as a well-remembered voice fell on his ears. His head jerked up and he stared in astonishment at Kathryn O'Keefe, in starched white apron and neat cap.

"What the hell—" he stammered.

"Your order—sir," she broke in coldly, staring at and through him.

Diana watched the girl's trim figure as she moved toward the kitchen. "Quite attractive, if you like the type." Her voice was languid. "Isn't she the female barkeep?"

Tex grunted, brow furrowed. The glowing picture he had painted in his mind was blotted out by Kathryn O'Keefe's expressionless gaze. Why was it, he asked himself angrily, that she should make him feel like a kid stealing apples, without saying a word. It was none of her business if he ate a meal with Diana Cresswell. He had nothing to be ashamed of. He was under no obligation to the saloon keeper's freckled daughter. But a shadow had crept over the sun.

Despite Diana's bright chatter and the admiring glances directed toward the table by hotel guests streaming in for lunch, the Texan was gripped by a black mood.

The meal over, Kathryn bustled up.

"Will there be anything else?" she inquired tartly.

Tex shook his head, eyes averted.

She pulled a pencil from the thick rope of coppery hair coiled around her head, rapidly wrote the check and thrust it, face downward, beneath his plate.

Idly, he turned the slip of paper over . . . and crushed it in his hand with a smothered oath. Beneath the bold notation, "Luncheon $2" were the words, "I gamble she offered you a soft job on the Box-C—chasing horseflies—sucker!"

"You look annoyed, Tex!" exclaimed his companion. With an effort he contorted his features into a grin. "Touch of colic; canned oysters never did take kindly t' me."

Diana threaded through the tables toward the lobby, soaking in the admiration that shone in men's eyes as indifferently as the desert soaks up a spring shower. Tex strode behind.

Kathryn hurried past. He grabbed her arm. "What d'ye mean—sucker?" he demanded in a low voice.

"If you can't beat a man—buy him," she snapped. "Better hustle—the blonde beauty is waiting for her pet poodle." She snatched her arm free, defiant eyes meeting his, as he glowered down at her flushed features, and darted away.

A burly cowman, with granite features, rose from a rocker as Diana and Tex entered the lobby. The girl tripped toward him. "Oh, Dad, I'm so glad you're in town. Tex and I have been talking and I told him you were willing to bury the hatchet." Laughing, she grasped the arms of both men. "Now shake hands and make up, like nice boys!"

Slowly the cowman extended his right hand, but Tex stood stiff and still, eyes clouded.

"I told Tex you needed a good man at Bitter River," the girl gushed. "Now's the time to talk business."

The sheriff's fingers twitched. Diana pulled his right arm forward. Then the thought of Kathryn's contemptuous eyes steeled him. His muscles tautened and his arm remained unmovable.

"Reckon Miss Diana got the wrong idea, Colonel," he drawled. "I aim t' stick around Hanging Wells—and I'm enforcin' the law, regardless."

The girl gasped in amazement. "Why, Tex!" Then swiftly, "It's that girl!"

Cresswell's arm dropped back to his side. "So yuh figger you kin buck the Box-C?" he rasped. "Then chew on this! Ef you don't turn in thet badge 'fore sundown I'll charge yuh with holding up the Tucson stage and runnin' with the Scarface gang—and I'll have Diana here testify under oath."

CHAPTER 14

For fleeting moments the Texan stood petrified, stunned by the shock of Cresswell's harsh threat. As its implications flashed through his mind he felt as though he stood on the brink of a gaping chasm, unable to pull back, compelled to step forward and plunge into the abyss.

Diana's evidence would convict him. She could testify that he had held up the stage with Scarface and his cohorts. Cresswell could throw out a dragnet that would pull in the other passengers and they would add their testimony. The Wells Fargo shotgun guard had been killed—that meant a murder charge, and the rope.

The ruthless Box-C boss had him hog-tied. There was only one faint gleam of hope. Stiffly, Tex jerked around to face Diana. The blonde's cheeks were no longer dimpled, her lips smiling. Pale face as cold as marble, she met his scrutiny, lips pressed in a thin straight line.

"Would yuh testify?" he asked, and read the answer in her cold blue eyes.

With a hopeless shrug the sheriff turned away.

"Wait!" Diana's clear-cut summons arrested him. "Don't be a fool, Tex," she urged, as cool as an icicle. "This is cow country. If you are not for us you must be against us—and we will crush every petty nester and sneak-thief who tried to steal our land. Come in with us—your own kind—now! Tomorrow will be too late."

Some inborn streak of obstinacy sealed the Texan's lips, or perhaps it was the memory of Pat O'Keefe's spunky daughter. His dark eyes traveled over Diana Cresswell, from the soft tanned leather of her handmade riding boots to the chiseled beauty of her features. He saw her no longer as an alluring piece of femininity, a ravishing beauty around whom he had woven roseate dreams, but as a heartless tool of the Box-C, in whose eyes he was no more than an undesirable obstacle to her father's ambitions.

Slowly, deliberately, he turned his back on them and strode out into the street.

He was through as sheriff of Hanging Wells, that was plain. There was a rope around his neck, grisly legacy of a thoughtless past, and Colonel Cresswell held the slack. His lips curled in a cynical smile as he moved along the plankwalk. An hour back he walked with his head on a level with the stars; now he was down in the dirt. Whichever way he turned he was faced by a black wall of hopelessness.

At the intersection, he paused as the Concha Copper Company's wagon, with its jingling escort of mounted men, rattled up to the bank. Another payroll was going out. What was it to him, anyway? He'd turn in his badge before the sun sank behind the Smokies. What then? Engrossed in his thoughts, he walked on, and on.

Removed from the floating dust and the elbowing groups at saloons and stores, the Hangman's Tree stood in solitary grandeur at the end of town, thrusting its gnarled branches high. The bench that girded its mighty trunk was deserted. Grateful for the shade and solitude, the despondent Texan sank down upon the seat. Set opposite, in the quiet tranquility of a grove of cottonwood, stood the little wooden church, silent and apparently deserted. But the perplexed sheriff, slumped in the shade of the mighty tree, noted that women, dark-skinned and white, continually slipped through its open door.

Tex's gloomy eyes lightened as a trim figure tripped lightly past yellow adobes and gray frame structures. The light faded when she darted a quick glance at the lonely form by the tree and stepped inside the house of worship without another look his way.

Another double-crossing female, thought the Texan despondently, as he watched Kathryn O'Keefe disappear into the quiet obscurity of the church. Played up to the law and banked a cut of the looted gold. What a hell of a town Hanging Wells had turned out to be!

Moodily, he rolled and smoked cigarette after cigarette, pondering upon his predicament and searching for a ray of light—in vain.

A girl's crisp voice jerked him back to alertness. Kathryn was poised before him, gazing at his somber features wih puzzled eyes.

"You got smallpox or something?" she inquired caustically.

"Nope, jest plain disgusted with life in general."

"Well, well! And you looked like you were sitting on top of the world back in the hotel." Her voice was cutting. "You and that blue-eyed blonde! So she turned you down! Cheer up, you'll feel better tomorrow."

"I done turned the Box-C down," flung back Tex, "and I won't be around tomorrow."

"No?" Her brow furrowed.

"Nope, I gotta turn in my badge afore sundown, then I reckon I'll vamoose."

"Whatever do you mean, Tex?" Her tone changed, softened. She sat down beside him.

"Cresswell's got me roped and hog-tied. It's throw in with the Box-C or be thrown out."

"But how on earth—" she began.

He stopped her with a swift gesture of his clenched fist. "I hit a crooked trail, way back, and Cresswell's wise. Thet gal of his kin fit a noose around my neck any time she wants."

"Oh!" Kathryn's voice was subdued, but there was a new light shining in her eyes. "Isn't there any way out?"

"Nope." His voice was leaded. "Guess I'll hit the trail f'r the border."

"And ride with the renegades! Oh, Tex, you're not that kind of man."

"Wal, what else kin I do?" he challenged.

"Face it out!" Her voice rang. "You've made good in Hanging Wells. Everyone respects you. You foiled the bank holdup, you saved the payroll and you arrested Monte Moreland right in the midst of the Box-C crew. Dad says you're even a better sheriff than Dan Cummings."

"Ain't no use," he replied tonelessly. "Least I kin draw is a term in Tucson pen, and I don't crave t' plait hair bridles." He dragged to his feet. "Reckon I'll turn in this star and punch the breeze."

"Wait, Tex!" she begged. "Give me time to talk to Dad. Colonel Cresswell may rod Smoky Valley but he doesn't run Hanging Wells."

Jaw set stubbornly, Tex moved upstreet with long strides, while the girl almost ran to keep pace with him. "Didn't Cresswell give you 'til sundown?" she panted.

He nodded.

"Then at least wait until then. Please, Tex—for me!"

"Ef you say so," he returned wearily.

"Tex!" Heinemann's excited shout rang across the street as they drew abreast of the bank. Hatless, the bank manager ran toward them, waving his arms frenziedly. A bespurred rider, dust-coated and haggard, dogged him.

He stumbled up to the sheriff, gasping for breath. "Those damned bandits are at work again," he jerked out. "They're attacking the payroll wagon. This man just brought the news. We've got to get some guns out there—quick!"

Tex forgot his troubles in the urge for action. He swung to the trail-worn rider. "Where's the fracas?"

"Fourteen, fifteen miles out—in the barrens."

"Yore pards holdin' 'em?"

"They was, when I hit f'r town."

"Git yourself a fresh hoss from the livery." Tex shouted the last words over his shoulder as he ran toward the nearest saloon. In ten minutes he had assembled a posse of punchers from the Lazy Y, Terrapin, Triple C and other ranches south and east of town. With a dozen eager waddies pounding at his back, he cantered out of town beside the messenger.

As they hit westward, toward the smelter's
eternal smoke blotch, he learned that the wagon
had pulled up for a road block. Before the escorting riders could roll the obstructing rocks away,
hidden desperadoes had dropped the team's two
leaders and wounded the driver. The guards had
gone to earth around the crippled wagon and were
trading lead with the bandits when the messenger
had taken a long chance, swung into leather and
broke through.

Pushing their mounts hard, the posse rode into
the sinking sun. For an hour they streaked across
the flats and into the foothills, pausing only to ease
their hard-breathing ponies. Swiftly, the terrain
changed. Grass gave way to bunched cacti, smooth
rolling hills to ragged granite outcrops and barren
ravines. Their ponies' hooves rang upon hard rock
as they clattered through an arid wilderness,
scarred by eroding buttes and treeless canyons.

"Ain't we about hit the spot?" inquired Tex,
swinging toward the guide, who rode at his side.
The other's intent eyes were focused up-trail, where
the wagon road wound up the ragged slopes to a
notch in a frowning bastion that blocked out the
setting sun.

"Danged close, but I can't hear no gunfire!" returned the rider uneasily.

The significance of the guide's words darkened
the sheriff's eyes, squinted against the blinding sun-
rays that glinted from naked rock and patched
white alkali.

Movement against the curving double ribbon of
gray-white dust that marked the wagon road drew
a quick exclamation from Tex. He shouted a warn-

ing to the men trailing behind, pulled down to a trot.

"Bunch of jaspers afoot," observed the guide. A few minutes later he ripped out an oath. "B'gawd, it's the boys!"

A weary file of footsore men, eyes shot with red from long staring over gunsights, faces bitter with the ignominy of defeat, limped down the rough road in high-heeled riding boots. Around the head of one was wrapped a bloodied bandanna, another's arm was supported in a rough sling, a third pulled himself along with a stiffened leg.

As the posse drew near, Tex noted that none of the trail-stained men wore gun-belts.

"How come you're afoot?" yelled the guide, as the possemen surged around the strangers.

Tex guessed the answer before it was given.

"Shells ran out," growled a sandy-haired man with tired eyes. "Them galoots grabbed our hosses and guns. There ain't much left of the payroll, outside the box."

"Set down and rest yore legs," directed Tex. "We'll be back pronto."

Spurring the buckskin, he hit toward the notch, silhouetted against the darkening sky ahead. Sparks aplenty flew from iron-shod hooves as the punchers, thirsting for action, urged their mounts upward in his wake.

Breasting the summit, Tex gazed down into a long, shallow depression, jumbled with huge boulders and carpeted with frosty cholla. Here was ideal cover for a thousand men. Not a mile distant stood a deserted wagon, outlined by the dying sun. Riderless ponies, stirrups swinging, nosed among the rocks or drifted around the wagon.

The sheriff told two men to round up the ponies, and headed for the wagon. The story of the attack was plain from the glittering shell cases littered around the forlorn vehicle, with its cut traces and two dead horses; the still forms of sprawled gray-shirted men; the splintered express box.

"What'll we do, Tex?" shouted a waddy. "Hit the trail of them gordamned bushwhackers?"

"Find it?" returned the sheriff laconically. With a sweep of the arm he indicated the wilderness of serried rock. "We'd stand a better chance of locating an ant in a straw stack than bumping up against the gents who grabbed thet payroll. They're scattered to hell-and-gone."

An army of shadows marched silently over the valley as the possemen piled rocks on the bodies of the dead men. In the gray twilight they backtrailed, leading the riderless ponies. The dejected payroll guards thankfully climbed into leather again and the cavalcade headed through the darkening solitude toward Hanging Wells.

Like lustrous pearls, the thick-clustered stars glowed softly as the shadowy bunch of horsemen crept across the mesquite flats and the lights of town pricked the darkness ahead. A spooky posseman dabbed for his gun when a lone rider materialized ghostlike from the gloom. His hand dropped hastily away as a girl's voice hailed them, "Is the sheriff there?"

Tex spurred ahead. Close at hand to Kathryn O'Keefe's small form was perched on a calico pony.

"I must speak to you—alone," she whispered

huskily, with a quick glance at the advancing horsemen.

"Keep a-goin' boys!" yelled Tex, pulling to one side, the girl tailing him. Together, they watched the bunched riders jog past and blend with the night.

"What's the trouble?" asked the sheriff. Then he remembered Cresswell's threat of exposure, which had been crowded from his mind by the holdup. "The Colonel gunnin' f'r me?"

"No, worse than that." The girl's voice was strained and anxious. "They are waiting to arrest you."

"Arrest me! What for?"

"Looting the payroll."

"Are you loco?" he snapped incredulously.

"Never so sane in my life," she returned quietly. "Monte Moreland rode into town at sundown and got the leading citizens together in the bank. Dad was there. Moreland said he had learned you were working hand in hand with the payroll bandits. To prove it, he challenged them to search your shack. They found a saddle bag stuffed with gold coin in the stove. Then the Colonel claimed he could prove you rode with the Scarface gang. They've made Plug Hawkins sheriff, and they're waiting for you —now."

CHAPTER 15

"When the Box-C bunch set out t' git a man, they sure ain't finicky," commented Tex ironically. "They ain't got the sand t' draw on him, so they knife him in the back. I reckon they'd stick wolf pison in his flapjack flour if that failed."

"Monte Moreland's a beast!" Kathryn declared vehemently. She eyed the Texan, dim in the starlight. "What are you going to do?"

"Hide out, I guess."

"You won't ride—for the border?" she ventured.

"Nope!" Tex's voice was harsh. "I aim t' stick around 'til we straighten out this payroll lootin'. I gotta talk with Moreland, too—with lead."

The girl heeled her pony and drifted close. She lifted a canteen, swung from her saddle horn, and a half-filled gunnysack and extended them to the lank Texan, set straight in the saddle.

He chuckled as he transferred them to his own saddle horn. "Chow! Wal, you forgot one thing."

"What?" she demanded in quick surprise.

Tex leaned forward. His long arm encircled Kathryn's waist and swept her out of the saddle. She struggled fiercely as he lifted her clear and pulled her tight against him. His lips sought hers and, of a sudden, her struggles ceased and she lay limp against him.

136

Gently, he lowered her to the ground.

"You'll come back?" Choked with emotion, the low-spoken question reached his ears.

"What—to the pen?" he asked moodily.

"We'll straighten this out. I—I need you, Tex," she pleaded.

"Where did them forty double eagles come from?" Abruptly, he shot the unexpected question.

Frowning, he stared down at the girl's white, blurred features.

"Over the bar." Her voice was faint, defiant.

"Would yuh take yore dyin' oath on that?" he demanded roughly.

Lips locked, she stood still as a statue.

With angry growl, he whirled the buckskin, drove home the steel and pounded into the night.

Paul Heinemann, manager of the Concha County Bank, was a man of method. Each evening he ate precisely at seven. Then, when the withered Piute squaw who served him as housekeeper cleared the table and washed dishes, he sat on the little porch in front of the white-painted bungalow and smoked a meditative cigar. After which, he lit the ornate oil lamp in the living room and read the "Concha County Record," or a book.

This evening he was in no mood to enjoy Mark Twain's drolleries. Sensation had crowded upon sensation since the sun last rose. Despite a heavily armed guard, the Concha Copper Company's payroll had again been looted. And what was even more surprising, Tex Tevis, the lean, sober-faced Texan who had tricked the bandits the previous month, had been denounced by Moreland of the Box-C as a slick crook, while Colonel Cresswell

sided with his foreman and declared he had posi-
tive proof that Tevis ran with the Scarface gang.
Doubtless by now, reflected the bank manager, the
Texan once more was caged in a courthouse cell.

Drawing hard on his cigar, Heinemann relaxed
in the comfortable rocker and reviewed the two
years he had spent in Hanging Wells. Poor health
had driven him to seek the pure Arizona air; that
health was now restored. What did this bleak,
brutal cowtown hold for a civilized man? Burning
heat in summer, raging blizzard in winter, with the
ever-present chance of a bullet from some crazy
bank robber. In the cities were theaters, clubs, a
hundred refinements of which these hard-riding,
tough-living cowmen knew nothing. Irritably he
tapped the white ash from his cigar and scattered it
with a polished shoe.

From the darkness, a voice, cold and low-
pitched, stiffened him into immobility. "I got yuh
covered, Heinemann, set quiet!"

The cigar dropped from the banker's slackened
lips; stiff with fear, his fingers gripped the arms of
the rocker. No more than a shadow in the obscurity, a figure clambered over the porch rail and stood
outlined beside it, gazing down at Heinemann's
taut form.

The banker moistened his dry lips. "Tevis!" His
voice quavered.

"Tex t' you," grunted the visitor. "I hear there's
a warrant out for me, robbery with violence. Who
swore to it?"

Heinemann cleared his throat, glanced helplessly
around. From inside the house came the tinkle of
gathered dishes. Friendly lights gleamed from
nearby houses. The banker suppressed a panicky

urge to yell frantically for aid—he had heard of the Texan's gun speed.

"I did," he croaked, cold sweat beading on his white forehead.

"On what evidence?"

"They found the gold in your cabin and Colonel Cresswell swears you ran with the Scarface gang."

"Who first pointed the finger at me?" persisted the questioner.

"Monte Moreland."

"And I gamble he led the way to my shack."

"Yes," agreed the banker, breathing deep.

"Was the gold marked?"

"Every coin."

"That settles Moreland's hash," commented Tex, with grim satisfaction. "He planted that gold, Heinemann, and you know where he got it. As f'r Cresswell, that range hog's wadin' in muddy water —he'll bog down. Guess that's all. So long!"

He vaulted the rail and evaporated into the night. For some moments, the bank manager sat immovable, then he rose shakily, entered the house and poured himself a stiff peg of raw whiskey. A very unusual proceeding!

Neither Heinemann nor his nocturnal visitor saw a bearded figure flattened on the ground beside the porch. The tails of his shoddy frock coat were tied in a huge knot to facilitate easy movement. His eager ears took in every word of the brief conversation. When the dull clip-clop of Tex's pony died in the distance, he rose and moved away, as silently and gracefully as a prowling panther.

Trail-stained and unshaven, Tex sat the buckskin on a shoulder of the undulating hills that fringed the Barrens, and gazed dreamily into a gem-like valley. A great square mesa formed its further boundary, rising in multi-colored strata of rock high above the surrounding hills. A rippling stream curved down its length, bordered with drooping willows and quaking aspen. Quail piped in the verdant grass and antelope slid like shadows through the chaparral. In a clearing at the foot of the butte a rectangle of charred timbers marked the site of a cabin. Close by, a pole corral still stood intact, while more blackened timbers showed where a barn had once stood.

Slowly the Texan built a smoke as he feasted his eyes on the spot which he and his brother had homesteaded with such high hopes—hopes that were ruthlessly smashed by Box-C guns.

Drawing upon the tube of tobacco, he saw in his mind's eye another cabin, larger, longer, logs freshly peeled and neatly notched. Fat steers grazing on the rich pasture. He saw, too, a girl with coppery hair standing at the cabin door, glad welcome shining in her dark eyes.

With a growl, he crushed the cigarette against the horn and jerked the buckskin around. A fool dream, with Kathryn O'Keefe tied into the outlaw set-up and he a wanted man, dodging a warrant!

For days Tex had combed the Barrens, hunting for a trace of the outlaw gang. Somewhere, he was convinced, they had a hideout, where they went to earth between raids and gathered to share the booty. His search had been in vain. Not a human being or the smoke of a campfire had he sighted in the waterless chaos of canyons and gulches, eroding buttes and dry watercourses. Finally, tiring of the pitiless sun-glare and barren wilderness of tortured

rock, he had ridden northward—to refresh his eyes
and spirits by gazing at the fragment of paradise he
had once called his own—Indian Bluff.

Again he headed southward. Far off, to his right,
the smelter befouled the purity of the azure sky.
Ahead, the tawny hills rolled in mighty waves,
dashing against the rocky ramparts of the Smokies,
at the foot of which, like the fossilized surf of a
stormy ocean, they broke into the Barrens. Beyond
the purple-veiled hills on his left lay the great bowl
that was Smoky Valley.

Sunk in thought, the Texan threaded through the
hills. Another payroll, to replace the looted gold,
would soon be freighted from the county seat to
the Copper Company. Emboldened by their suc-
cess, he believed the bandits would strike again. If
he could not ferret out their hideaway, perhaps he
could trail them to it. Why not dog the payroll
wagon, dog the bandits if it were attacked?

With nightfall he pulled into a brushy ravine,
kindled a small fire and boiled a pannikin of coffee.
With bacon and beans, this tightened his belt. He
stamped out the embers of his fire, pulled off his
boots, rolled up in his slicker and slept.

Another day found him stretched out atop a
squat black butte that bordered the Barrens. Beneath, like a gliding serpent, curled the wagon
road, coiling out of the valley haze and snaking
into the maze of ravines that harbored the bandit
gang.

Two days he spent in solitary vigil when—half
dozing in the heat of forenoon—he glimpsed dust
plumes far out on the valley flats. Eagerly he
focused his glasses. Plain in the lens was the payroll
wagon, flanked by riders, while another bunch of

mounted men cantered behind.

Leisurely, the watcher descended. He had time to kill before the wagon and its escort hit the Barrens.

Screened by the brush, he watched the party clatter past, a full hour later. The Concha Copper Company was taking no chances this trip. Six armed men galloped on each side of the jouncing wagon. A dozen more were bunched in its rear.

When the lazy dust clouds that drifted in the wake of the party had settled, Tex swung into leather and jogged easily along the trail. Not much chance of a holdup this time, he reflected, for no gold-hungry renegades would be crazy enough to attack twenty-four armed men, plus the guards who rode the wagon.

For a while he drifted through the silent wilderness, destitute of life save for the buzzards, black dots circling high in the blue.

Then, from the rocky fastnesses ahead, came the short, sharp crack of a rifle. Before the echoes rumbled away, a veritable drumfire from rifles and six-guns lashed the still air, reverberating among the cliffs and canyons in a devil's symphony.

"Git a wiggle on!" snapped Tex to the lazily stepping buckskin. "They sure hit the jackpot!"

Streaking between the ruts of the wagon road, he flashed through a gloomy defile between beetling escarpments. Close ahead, but out of sight, guns thundered in ear-splitting chorus.

The confining walls dropped away and the pursuing rider yanked his pony to an abrupt halt. A cup-like depression lay at his feet, through which the wagon road angled, to slant up again to another narrow defile.

Beneath his breath he cursed the ingenuity of the bandits as his eyes darted over the scene of battle. The hood of the wagon was visible behind a jumble of boulders that blocked the mouth of the defile. One huge boulder had crashed upon the wagon bed, smashed the hood and lay, half-exposed.

The hold-up gang had allowed the wagon to enter the narrow passageway, then rolled down an avalanche of rock—cutting off the majority of the riders who formed its guard. Probably, mused Tex, the defile was also blocked so that the wagon could move neither ahead nor back.

Blocked off, raked by the fire of bandits from the cliffs above, the escort crouched behind boulders or spread-eagled in the stunted brush, while their ponies wandered unattended.

It was a one-sided battle and it was obvious to the tight-lipped Texan that the end could not long be delayed. Wedged in the defile, the wagon guards were at the mercy of the bandits on the ledges high over their heads. The men spread over the basin, firing upward at will-of-the-wisp flashes, blinded by the scorching sun and laced by renegade lead, were in a hopeless position. Watching, the Texan planned a course of action.

Tex wheeled and withdrew into the shelter of the canyon behind him. His job was to outflank the renegades before they made their getaway, and he had little time to spare.

Emerging into the sunlight at the canyon's further end, he searched his surroundings. Impassable cliffs rose to his left. On the right the terrain was cut into a chaos of canyons. He kneed the buckskin toward the canyons, intent upon circling behind the battling men, whose gunfire still rattled and thundered in his rear.

At a gallop, he tore through treeless canyons, crossed talus-littered benches, circled the rugged flanks of towering buttes. In that rockbound maze, he could not do more than endeavor to head in a general direction and follow any accessible trail.

The thunder of the guns grew fainter and more distant as he penetrated further into the arid fastnesses. Ever pressing westward, he urged his laboring pony to greater speed. Once the gunfire died, his one guide to the location of the renegades would be gone.

Of a sudden, his fears were realized. Sullen silence cloaked the crags. No sound arose save the metallic ringing of the buckskin's hooves upon rock and the snorting whistle of air through its widely distended nostrils.

He reined down the hard-breathing pony, listened with strained ears, but not a murmur disturbed the serenity of the solitudes.

Bitter disappointment welled up within the Texan; either the fracas had ended and the bandits had again disappeared into the vastness with their loot, or he had been thrown far off his trail in the tangle of canyons.

Wearily he shook his pony into a trot and headed westward. The terrain flattened into a succession of low-lying ridges, out of which isolated mesas bulked high, like islands in a granite sea.

Tex had long since given up hope of locating the scene of the holdup; he was hopelessly lost in the twisted chaos of the untracked barrens. But fate again took a hand.

Idly studying the vistas ahead as he jogged

along, the Texan glimpsed a bunch of fast-moving horsemen as they topped a ridge, riding northward. As he watched, they disappeared—to creep into view again as they breasted another ridge.

With renewed hope, he pricked his pony into a gallop, cutting off at an angle that would intercept the strangers.

Seeking low ground to avoid discovery, he streaked northwest for thirty minutes or more, then ground-hitched the hard-breathing pony and cautiously crept up the steep flank of a ridge, searching for further sign of the horsemen.

Not a mile distant, the riders angled across a bench. He dropped down and again hit leather, convinced that this was the bandit gang. Keeping to the canyons, he spurred in their wake.

In a succession of benches, the terrain slanted upward toward a great irregular wall of rock that stretched across his front like the bastion of a mighty fortress.

Strung out in single file, the riders—a dozen or more—angled up toward the wall. Far below them, compelled to chance discovery, the Texan followed.

As his pony panted up the slopes, Tex sighted a cleft in the cliff wall, toward which the dark blobs that were his quarry were heading. One by one they reached the cleft and disappeared from view.

Long after they had vanished, Tex reached the foot of the wall and reined up, gazing doubtfully into a narrow pass.

Its gloomy portals were no more than a slit in the sundered rock, through which two men could not have ridden abreast. It was darkened by the stark walls upthrust on either side. The talus of centuries had spilled into it—hoofmarks were plain upon the heaped dust.

What lay beyond the shadowed cut? Was it the entrance to the long-sought hideout, or merely a pass to wilder country beyond?

Tex blew the dust from his gun, twirled the cylinder, and dropped it back into the holster. Then he headed into the gloomy passage. . . . Roaring like a cannon in the confined space, a gun spat red fire not fifty paces ahead.

CHAPTER 16

Tex instinctively ducked as the powder flash flared through the gloom of the narrow cut. A slug ricocheted off the rock wall beside him and whined into space. While the roar of the explosion yet pounded against his eardrums, the Texan's gun was barking, splashing hot lead in the direction of his unseen assailant.

While bullets whizzed by, he backed the buckskin, gained the open and spurred his pony clear of the entrance, out of his opponent's range of fire.

Vaulting out of leather, he trailed the reins and edged to the side of the dark slot, plugging fresh loads into his forty-five.

Tensed, he waited, but there was no further sign of life in the gloomy cut. The hombre inside, reflected Tex wryly, held all the aces. He was concealed by the darkness, maybe hunched behind cover. Any man trying to force his way through made a clear-cut target against the brilliance of the sky behind him. He had just escaped death only by a miracle. It would be suicide to tempt fate again.

Belly-flat, he wormed forward, pushed his Stetson ahead as though he were cautiously peering into the cut. It was a time-worn trick, but there was a chance the hidden marksman might snap at the bait.

He did! The Stetson jerked as a rifle spat viciously. Mingled with the reverberating report, a high-pitched Apache yell echoed eerily.

Tex's eyes gleamed as he set the hat, neatly bored through the crown, on his head. That was Moreland's bloodcurdling yell. He had heard it on the bloody night when a Box-C crew had blasted his brother and burned his ranch. It crowned his suspicions with conviction. The Box-C foreman ran with the renegade gang.

He squinted toward the sun, a white ball arcing down to the horizon. It would be a full three hours before dark, a three-hour wait before night shrouded his movements and he could make an attempt to force his way into the cut.

After loosening and rocking the heavy double-cinched Texas saddle on the buckskin, he rolled a smoke and leisurely examined the craggy wall that towered high above. It rose almost perpendicular, smoothed by centuries of storm, an unclimbable barrier. He hunkered comfortably at its foot and composed himself to wait.

Night flung a purple mantle over the Barrens, softening its stark ugliness and clothing the fading ridges with mystery. Starry hosts pinpointed the heavens, glowing brighter as the day waned.

Tex rose, stretched, and eyed the dark shadow that marked the mouth of the cut. The time had arrived to call Moreland's hand.

Unbuckling his spurs, he hung them from the saddle horn, then cat-toed to the black gap. Crouched low, he listened, then, fingers brushing his gun butt, foot by foot he eased into the chasm of darkness.

Left hand groping the wall, Tex worked blindly forward, high-heeled riding boots slipping and sliding on the heaped talus. But no thundering onslaught disputed his progress.

Thirty paces ahead, the passage slanted to the right. Feeling his way like a blind man, ever alert for a sudden attack by a hidden foe, Tex fingered his way into the depths. A quotation of the Preacher's buzzed through his brain. "Walk in darkness and the shadow of death."

Faint light glowed ahead. Tex quickened his pace. In a few minutes he stood at the further end of the cut, gazing out upon a wide, shadowed canyon, into which a narrow trail snaked down.

A disgusted growl left his throat. "Moreland sure fooled me," he murmured. "While I was settin' round like a sick cow, them coyotes were pounding leather."

He scrambled back through the passageway, forked his pony and headed down toward the canyons. A feeling of frustration leaded his spirits. Moreland had outfoxed the payroll guard and fooled him. By now the renegades had gone to earth in some inaccessible hideaway. He had the evidence he sought—Moreland was linked with the payroll looters—but what use was it? He was a fugitive, disgraced and discredited. Against the Box-C foreman, backed by the all-powerful Colonel Cresswell, he was helpless. He needed proof, proof that would convince the citizens of Hanging Wells, and where could he get it?

Depressed, and bedeviled by the perversity of fate, he made dry camp in a sheltered coulee and rolled up in his slicker for the night.

Dawn found the Texan heading eastward, to-

ward Smoky Valley and the Box-C. In the midnight hours he had pondered his problem and
found but one solution—shoot it out with the
dark-skinned foreman. He had debts aplenty to
pay—debts that could only be wiped out by gun-
smoke.

It was noon before the sprawling Box-C spread
lay before him. Eyes alert for sight of his enemy, he
rounded the house and rode for the barns.

Not a puncher moved around the ranch. With
growing amazement, Tex slipped out of leather,
pushed open the bunkhouse door and peered inside. It was deserted. Blankets were piled in the
double tier of bunks that lined the walls. A chair
was upset and a deck of cards spilled over the table
edge.

"Looks like they vamoosed sudden," mused the
Texan. Leading his pony, he headed for the house,
hammered on the door with his gun butt.

A heavy step sounded inside and the door jerked
open. Anger smoldering in his cold eyes, Colonel
Cresswell faced him.

"Monte Moreland around?" demanded Tex
brusquely.

"Nope!" roared the Colonel. "The dogblasted
coyote done took off with my gal."

"And a sack of Concha Copper Company gold,"
added Tex. "Yore crew fogged, too?"

They're huntin' Moreland. I told 'em t' ride wide
of the Box-C until they plug thet double-crossin'
sheepherder."

"Kinda fond of the gal, ain't yuh?" Tex eyed the
grizzled Colonel thoughtfully. It was plain, from
the cowman's furrowed brow and weary sag of the
shoulders, that he was hard hit.

"Sooner lose my right arm," admitted Cresswell. Then, with a return of his belligerency, "What's it t' you?"

"I'd kinda like t' make a trade," returned Tex slowly, watching Cresswell through narrowed eyes. "I'm gunnin' f'r Moreland. Ef I git him and bring the gal back, will yuh throw Smoky Valley open f'r homesteadin'?"

Cresswell snorted like an angry bull, stepped back and swung the heavy door in the Texan's face.

Tex's boot jammed it. "Think again!" he grated. "Is yore gal worth more'n a few lousy acres?"

Their eyes battled. The cowman hesitated, bit his lip, then nodded reluctantly. "It's a deal!" he grunted.

Tex thought hard as he rode away from the silent ranch. If Moreland had kidnaped Cresswell's daughter and toted a stack of looted gold, his first thought would be to place himself out of reach of the law. That meant crossing the border. Once over he would be safe—beyond the reach of quick-shooting posses and legal processes.

Between Smoky Valley and the border stretched seventy miles of desert. Apache Wells, fifty miles to the south, offered the only water. It was a long, punishing ride. Moreland and the girl could not reach the Wells before sundown, which meant a layover for the night. That, reasoned Tex, gave him a chance to overtake them. It was a gamble, a three to one shot. Moreland might have hit west across the Smokies or east for New Mexico. But the Texan determined to play his hunch, and headed the buckskin southward.

Imperceptibly, the pasture land, seamed with

cowpaths, fringed into desert. Easing his pony along at a steady jog-trot, the Texan left the rolling swales and grazing steers of Smoky Valley behind and emerged upon a sun-baked waste of sage. This, too, gave place to soft yielding sand, out of which protruded squat buttes and huge fragments of smooth-polished basalt. Here bunched the malignant thousand-spined cholla. Majestic saguaros thrust their fluted columns high. White-plumed tufts of Spanish bayonet mingled with the scarlet-hued ocotillo. Here, too, disintegrating skeletons and sun-dried carcasses of cows told of the grisly specter that ever hovers over the waterless wastes. Rattlers slithered beneath shady rocks. Black buzzards circled lazily against the blue.

Wreathed in a choking fog of dust, horse and rider crept slowly across the arid waste, swerving around impassible thickets of prickly pear, dropping down the crumbling banks of boulder-littered washes, thudding across glassy stretches of dirty-white alkali.

The day wore on. Tex reined up the buckskin, grayed with dust, trickled the remaining contents of his canteen into the crown of his Stetson and held it beneath the pony's eager muzzle. Again he hit leather, eyes searching the purpled vistas ahead as sun dropped toward the distant mountains, simmering through the heat waves.

Far ahead, no more than a faint shadow, obscured by whirling dust devils, a stark finger of rock pointed upward from the desert's maw. Tex grunted with satisfaction as he squinted with red-rimmed eyes. It was Apache Butte, at the foot of which were rock-ribbed basins of precious water . . . and, if the gods smiled, his quarry.

The butte was still distant when night blanketed the desert and the solitary rider nursed his wearying pony through the thorned bush.

Like a glowing cigarette, a red spark pricked through the darkness. Tex's aching eyes brightened; someone was camping at the Wells.

There was little chaparral around the waterhole. At the foot of the towering butte, water seeped into a succession of depressions in the rock; cold, clear water from a spring that never failed.

As the Texan drew closer, two figures, moving around the flickering fire, were plain. Circling, he placed the bulk of the butte between himself and the campers. Drifting close, he slid out of leather and tied the pony to the trunk of a twisted mesquite. Then, like an Indian, he stole through the stunted desert growth.

Stretched behind a clump of galleta grass not fifty paces from the campfire, Tex watched with growing surprise. Moreland and Diana Cresswell sat side by side, propped against their saddles, eyeing the spears of flame that leaped high from the mesquite fire. The girl's laughing voice and Moreland's deep-voiced replies floated out into the silent desert.

This girl was no unwilling prisoner, decided the Texan, kidnaped by a ruthless desperado. She acted more like a bride on a honeymoon trip. Well, he decided grimly, the Box-C foreman had other charges to face besides kidnaping and it was his job to take him back—dead or alive.

He straightened, paced slowly toward the crackling fire. Moreland heard him first. The foreman swiftly gestured his companion to silence. Leaping to his feet, he whirled, glimpsed the silent, oncoming figure. Diana leaned forward and threw an armful of dead brush on the fire. It blazed high, bathing the scene in bright light.

"Wal, ef it ain't the nester, hornin' in agen!" grated Moreland, clapping his hand on the butt of the gun sagging from his waist.

Tex stopped short, a dozen paces distant.

"So yuh grabbed the gold and the gal!" he commented tersely.

Moreland's white teeth gleamed in the firelight as they were bared in a mirthless grin. "What are yuh goin' t' do about it?"

"I'm takin' you back."

The foreman laughed, a short bitter laugh that was half sneer. "You and who else? You ain't never goin' back, nester!"

With the last word his gun jumped up and out. He was fast, but not so fast as the Texan. As his weapon arced down, Tex's holster jerked up and lanced flame. The slug bedded in Moreland's right shoulder. Spun half around by the force of the impact, he shifted his iron with a lightning-like gesture from right hand to left. Again, the Texan's gun hammered him. Smashing into his left hand, clutching the uplifted gun, the bullet tore off his thumb and ranged upward, plowing through his forearm.

Moreland's six-gun flew sideways, clanged flatly on the rock. Blood swiftly stained his shirt from the wound in his shoulder and ran scarlet from his smashed left hand. Moreland cursed in incoherent rage. Helpless and bloodied, he staggered toward his opponent.

"Hold it!" snapped Tex, still grasping the butt of his smoking iron. "I'll sink yuh next shot."

Intently watching the winged Box-C foreman, Tex forgot the girl. Her voice, cool and clear-cut, jerked his eyes from Moreland's swaying figure. "Drop that gun, Tex, or I'll drop you!"

Half crouched, blue eyes hard as twin sapphires, Diana Cresswell covered him with a stub-barreled derringer.

CHAPTER 17

At the girl's swift challenge, the Texan's head jerked around. Sardonically, he eyed the pointed gun and Diana's tight-set features behind it.

"Wal, ef that don't beat hell!" he ejaculated, making no effort to obey her crisp command.

"What do you mean?" she snapped, clenching the gun with an unwavering hand.

"Heah I sashay fifty miles over thet doggoned desert, because yore pa's breakin' his heart over his poor little rustled lamb, and she throws a gun on me. Is that nice?" His voice was ironical.

"My father never wasted a thought on anything except his infernal cows," she replied fiercely. "And, smartie, I was not kidnaped. I ran away with Monte. Now throw up your hands, pronto!"

Tex pulled a sack of makin's out of a vest pocket. "Ef you don't plug the holes in thet hombre," he commented dryly, "yo're liable t' have a stiff on yore hands." Confirming his words, Moreland, bleeding freely and blindly stumbling, tripped and sprawled headlong. Both arms useless, he lay writhing on the rocky ground, cursing impotently.

Diana hesitated, blue eyes sparkling frostily as she faced the impassive Texan. Then she thrust the derringer into her holster. With quick steps she hurried to the wounded man and sank on her knees beside the groaning, twisting figure.

Without ado, the girl flicked up her riding skirt and exposed a white petticoat.

"Lend me your knife?" she requested crisply.

Tex fished out his Barlow knife and snapped the blade open. Diana took it without a word and cut through the hem of the petticoat. Then she ripped the white muslin into strips, handing them one by one to the watching Texan.

Adroitly she cut away Moreland's sodden shirt, plugged and wrapped the wound in his shoulder. Next she bandaged the ragged stump of the foreman's thumb and his lacerated arm. The wounded man lay flat on his back, lips compressed, deep-set eyes glaring venomously at his assailant.

The job done, Diana rose to her feet, with blood-ied hands.

"I should have killed you," she informed Tex, cloudy eyes regarding Moreland's red-hued band-ages.

Tex's lips twisted. "Too late now!"

With quick consternation she fumbled for her gun. The holster was empty.

"You despicable thief!" As the words choked out of her throat, her eyes swiftly scrutinized the ground.

"I collected Moreland's iron, too," chuckled Tex. "Little lost lambs ain't fit t' be trusted with guns." He glanced toward the runaways' two ponies, picketed nearby. "Reckon I'll borrow them cayuses and drift. You might git notions. See yuh at sunup. Adios!"

Moreland cursed him fluently as he strode toward the animals but the girl merely watched—with eyes like rapiers.

Tex threaded through the thorny mesquite and lacy greasewood, leading the ponies to his own mount on the farther side of the butte. Then, weary from the long ride across the desert, he bedded down for the night.

As the sun silvered the cholla and gilded the woolly thunderheads resting on the squat shoulders of the distant Smokies, he saddled up and returned to the Wells, with the two ponies on the lead. In the chilly desert dawn, Diana was huddled over a blazing fire. Moreland, propped against a saddle, was haggard with pain and loss of blood. Neither, figured the Texan, had slept a wink.

With a cheery greeting, he dismounted. "Time t' pack, folks. Gotta hit f'r home."

Studiously ignoring him, the girl lifted her saddle and set it on her mare. Moreland swayed to his feet and glowered at the Texan, as the latter hefted his gear.

"Weighs more'n a sack of sand," commented Tex, setting the saddle on Moreland's sorrel. He cinched the rig tight, then unbuckled a saddle bag and pulled out a small bulging canvas sack.

"Keep yore long nose outa my stuff!" barked the foreman. Raging, he stepped forward.

"It's no use going on the prod, Monte," cut in Diana stonily, "and vile language doesn't help. We're defenseless against this cheap sneak-thief."

Tex shook the bag. The contents clinked musically.

"I'm gamblin' this is Concha Copper Company

gold," he commented. Untying the thong that secured the neck of the sack, he spilled a glittering cascade of gold coins into his spread palm, thumbed the nicks on their edges.

"Jest a dirty crook and killer!" he taunted. "I'll take these—f'r evidence." He stowed the gold in his own saddle bags and added another sack which further search revealed.

The girl mounted her pony and sat, fidgeting impatiently.

"You ride ahead, ma'am," advised Tex. "Moreland won't be along f'r awhile, mebbe he won't come at all."

"I don't understand!"

"Yuh don't have to!" flung back the Texan. "Vamoose!"

Diana's perplexed eyes searched his somber features. "What deviltry are you up to now?" she demanded. "I won't budge until Monte rides."

"Suits me!" he replied indifferently. "But gimme silence, in big gobs."

He turned to the bandaged foreman.

"You framed me, Moreland. Planted Concha Copper gold in my shack. I figgered you were crooked, but I didn't savvy you rode with the payroll gang until yesterday. Yore yell was a clear giveaway. That chunk of gold," he nodded toward his saddle bags, "cinches it. I'm givin' yuh a choice—spill the beans, ride back t' take yore medicine. Dumb up, and I'll leave yuh here. Mebbe some soft-hearted gent ull drift in. The odds are yuh won't see him—you'll be worm feed by then."

"You be damned!" snorted Moreland.

Tex shrugged, swung into leather, and grabbed the reins of the sorrel. "Let's go!"

Diana pulled back, face blanched. "You can't leave him—it's murder!"

"You talk t' me of murder!" Tex's even tone broke, became harsh in the stress of the anger that surged within him. "That coyote's pack has murdered a dozen payroll guards. He cut down my brother, and plugged Gawd knows how many nesters."

"In fair fight!" she flung back, cheeks blazing.

"Ef droppin' men from ambush is fair fightin', then thet fancy man of yours is some square shooter," raged the Texan. He dropped the sorrel's reins, kneed his pony against the girl's mount and seized its headstall.

In an intensity of fury, Diana flung herself at him like a wildcat, clawing at his face and hair with silent, white-toothed ferocity. The Texan's sombrero flew off. Four parallel scratches bloomed red, as the girl's nails raked his cheek.

He grabbed one arm, lifted his rope off the horn and dallied it around her wrist. Then he jerked her body forward, gripped her left arm and, in a trice, secured it to the other, and lashed both to the horn.

Helpless, she could do no more than twist and strain at the chafing rope.

Grasping the reins of her pony and the sorrel's, he heeled the buckskin and moved toward the desert.

Fifty paces distant he turned leisurely at Moreland's hoarse yelling.

"What's on yore mind?" he hailed.

"I'll talk, blast yuh f'r a lousy sheepherder!"

The Texan wheeled and, with his two led ponies and the roped girl, walked his buckskin back to the foreman.

He pulled up and coolly eyed Moreland's rage-distorted features. "What I need is a written confession," he ruminated, "but both yore flippers are out of action. Guess I gotta call on you as a witness," he grinned at the tight-lipped Diana. "Now, answer pronto, afore I change my mind. Did yuh ride with the gang thet rustled the Concha Copper payrolls?"

"Yep," muttered Moreland sullenly.

"And did yuh plant the gold in my shack?"

"Yep!"

"How come you're hittin' f'r the border?"

"What d'you think?" grated the foreman.

"Reckon thet's enough f'r now. We'll put it on paper when we git t' town." Tex swung to the ground. "Git a wiggle on! I'll give yuh a leg up and we'll drift."

Moreland hoisted into leather, the Texan untied the girl's rope-burned wrists and handed her the derringer. She thrust the gun into her holster and heeled the mare, heading northward, while Tex and his prisoner jogged behind.

Three dust-grimed riders on jaded ponies drifted down valley as the sun sank behind the Smokies. Moreland swayed in the saddle from exhaustion. Diana had dropped back and ridden at the tail of Tex's pony for a dozen miles. Her voice, sharp-edged with fatigue and tension, cut into a silence that had blanketed the hours. "I've got you covered, Tex. Pull up!"

Moreland shot a startled glance behind him. The Texan jogged on, unheeding.

"Stop, you fool, or I'll shoot!" There was no mistaking the deadly earnestness in the girl's high-pitched voice. "Reckon she's been working herself up to this for an hour or more," reflected Tex. But still he gave no sign.

The roar of the gun set Moreland's sorrel pitching and almost unseated the helpless prisoner. Tex held his pony down. As the gun roared again, he turned his head.

"Save yore ammunition, ma'am," he advised. "I dug the lead outa them cartridges last night." With a gesture of despair, the girl flung the useless gun into the grama beside the trail. The Texan reined up. "Reckon you kin locate the ranch now. Moreland and me's got business in town."

Diana spurred her pony ahead. Tex watched her swaying body as she breasted the swales, then swung eastward with his prisoner.

Moreland was on the brink of collapse when the pair reached Hanging Wells. Night had long since fallen and the town slept, save in the vicinity of the saloons. Supporting his prisoner in the saddle, Tex headed for the home of Doc Hoskins.

Stuck out from the rear of the peppery little doctor's square frame bungalow, like a tail from a tadpole, was a long low shack, lined with bunks, which the doctor proudly termed the hospital. It was seldom indeed that one or more of the bunks was not occupied by punchers recuperating from what was appropriately known as "lead poisoning."

With Moreland safely bedded down in the hospital, Tex rode past darkened houses toward Main Street. Light glimmered in the windows of the sheriff's office. The Texan tied his pony, mounted the familiar courthouse steps, a bag of looted gold dangling from each hand.

Gaunt old Dan Cummings sat at the spur-scratched desk. He masked the surprise that Tex's unexpected appearance must have evoked with a noncommittal grunt.

Eyes red-shot and chin stubbled, the Texan sank into a chair, dropped the heavy bags on the floor beside him and rolled a smoke.

Cummings slid open a desk drawer, produced a bottle and extended it to his visitor. Yuh look kind-a tickered out," he commented.

Tex thankfully tilted the bottle. The raw whiskey bit his throat and renewed energy flowed through his trail-weary body.

"Packin' a warrant f'r me?" he queried.

Cummings nodded, heavy-lidded eyes focused on his former deputy.

"Tear it up! I brought in the varmint who rodded the payroll gang, and here's his cut of the loot." He hefted the two sacks and dumped them on the desk.

"So yuh got Moreland!" murmured Cummings thoughtfully.

"How did yuh guess?"

"Thet dinero in your cabin was a plant, like I told the boys. Moreland pointed the finger at yuh, so he planted it. But he ain't the king-pin."

"I claim he is," snapped the saddle-sore Texan impatiently.

"You're barkin' up the wrong tree." Cummings' voice was decided.

"Then it's Colonel Cresswell!"

"Prove it!" challenged the sheriff.

"By Gawd, I will, afore I'm through," declared Tex irritably.

Cummings wriggled his bony frame more comfortably into the swivel chair. "Yuh ain't told me how yuh come t' grab Moreland," he prompted.

Tex sketched the story of his misadventure in the
Barrens, his visit to the Box-C and the long chase
across the desert.

"Yuh shoulda killed the bastard," commented
Cummings dryly, when Tex told of the gun fight at
Apache Wells.

"Dead men don't talk," returned the Texan
laconically.

For a while the sheriff sat silent, eyes hooded, as
he digested the news his former deputy had
brought.

"You go git some shuteye," he directed at
length. "I'll check yore story with Moreland
tomorrow. Then we'll take the testimony of the gal
—thet should cook his goose. I reckon we kin
squash thet warrant agenst you and stick a
deputy's badge on yore chest. Ef Moreland spills
his guts we'll hev work aplenty."

The sun was high when Tex awoke the next
morning. He fed his buckskin, pawing in the lean-
to against the rear of the shack, leisurely cooked
his breakfast and shaved.

By the time he rambled down to the office, Cummings had pulled out. Men eyed him curiously
when he drifted into The Double Eagle. An un-
familiar figure behind the bar reminded him that
Kathryn had changed her job. The O'Keefes lived
on a small spread south of town. He made a mental
note to ride out there—pronto.

He spent an hour over a bottle of beer, sitting by
the window smoking and eyeing the townsfolk as
they passed by. After days on the dodge, ever alert
for a bullet or a posse, the reeking saloon seemed a

corner of paradise. Moreland's confession had lifted a great weight off the Texan's mind. Yesterday he had been a hunted man, a price on his head and a warrant dogging every step. Today he was free, his deadly enemy was crushed, and—greatest triumph of all—Cresswell, the all-powerful cattle king, had agreed to allow homesteaders in Smoky Valley. Through the lazy drifting tobacco smoke, the Texan saw a neat little spread in the shadow of a mighty mesa, with fat steers feeding by a sparkling creek and a coppery-haired girl bustling around a peeled log cabin.

With jaunty step he again headed for the sheriff's office. The door was closed. He knuckled the panel and pushed it open. Three heads swiveled—Colonel Cresswell, Heinemann the bank manager and Sheriff Dan Cummings were in close confab.

Tex sensed from their expressionless stare that something was amiss. A cold chill blighted his rosy dreams. Covering his qualms with a grin, he inquired, "Got the confession all fixed up, Dan?"

"Nope," returned the sheriff shortly. "Moreland swears it's a pipe dream and the Colonel's gal seconds him. Claims they were ridin' down t' the Colonel's Bitter River ranch when you jumped 'em."

"How about the gold?" Tex's voice was tense.

"It was in your saddle bags," broke in Heinemann pointedly.

"Would I have rode t' town and dumped it on Cummings' desk ef I looted it?" demanded the Texan heatedly.

Heinemann shrugged his well-tailored shoulders. "It may have been a stratagem. I have no personal animosity, Tevis, but the Colonel swears he can

prove you were a member of the Scarface gang.
Marked gold was found hidden in your cabin. Yet
you expect us to believe the cock-and-bull story
Sheriff Cummings has repeated to us! It is your un-
supported word against the county's leading
rancher, his daughter and his foreman."

"What do you say?" Tightly, Tex fired the question at the poker-faced Cresswell.

"I side with Heinemann," rasped the cowman.
"Reckon I tangled my rope over Diana. The gal
claims she was ridin' down to our border ranch and
asked Monte t' mosey along."

"And the homestead deal is off?" The Texan's
voice was quiet—too quiet.

"You bet yore sweet life it is," roared Cresswell.
"The Box-C rods Smoky Valley."

Tex's features contorted in a mirthless travesty
of a grin that reflected the crash of his new-built
hopes. Bleak, his eyes met the sheriff's blank stare.

"So the warrant stands, Dan?"

Cummings nodded slowly.

Loose-hanging, the Texan's hand clamped upon
his gun butt. The swiveled holster snapped up.

"Reach, gents!" he ordered coldly.

CHAPTER 18

Heinemann's manicured hands strained ceilingward at the Texan's bleak order. Cummings's speculative eyes shuttled from the up-tilted gun to the hard line of Tex's lean jaw. Then he, too, elevated his arms. Cresswell kicked back his chair with an oath and leaped into action. He dabbed for his gun and brought it up in a flashing arc. Sidestepping behind the stiff, stretched banker, he clicked back the hammer of his iron and flung down over Heinemann's shoulder.

White-faced, the banker flinched as Tex whipped a slug past his ear. Cresswell's gun belched flame a split second later, but the Texan's slug had already punched through his wrist. His bullet ripped the floor boards and he growled like a maddened bear as the sagging gun slipped through his nerveless fingers and plunked to the floor. Although the bright blood from his smashed wrist splashed over Heinemann's pale face and besplattered his spotless shirt front, the banker stood as though petrified, staring eyes glued to the Texan's smoking iron.

Tex backed through the swirling powder smoke, eyes coldly alert. His heel hit the closed door. He fumbled behind his back with his left hand, fingered the knob and flung it open. Sliding swiftly outside, he bounded along the corridor and plunged down the courthouse steps to his waiting pony. Jerking the knotted reins loose, the Texan vaulted into leather and spurred the buckskin.

The pony's flying hooves struck sparks as it lunged forward. At that moment Sheriff Cummings banged through the courthouse door. His six-gun spat viciously as Tex leaned over the pony's withers, urging it to greater speed. The animal flashed from the hitch rail and the Texan heard Cummings's bullet drone high overhead. Another followed, wide of the mark. The fleeing rider grunted, more in disgust than relief. "They tole me Dan was death with a six-gun," he informed the madly galloping pony. "Hell, the old coot couldn't hit a haystack!"

Like a whirlwind, horse and rider streaked along the main street, passed outlying adobes and headed south along the brush-bordered wagon road.

Noon found the Texan lying at ease beneath the grateful shade of a spreading willow, six miles north of town. At his back, Rattlesnake Creek, a slow-flowing stream that looped through the valley, gurgled lazily. The pony cropped the lush grass at the water's edge. To elude capture, Tex had circled and no sign of a pursuing posse had as yet developed.

Despite his successful getaway, the Texan dolefully sucked on a cigarette. In a brief space his castle of dreams had tumbled down. Not three hours before, he reflected glumly, he had been sitting on top of the world, now he was once again on the dodge, with no future save a cell in Tucson.

Only one road to freedom remained and that lay south, toward the border. And Kathryn O'Keefe? Whether she was tainted with renegade gold or not, that girl had proved a real pard. Come hell or high water, decided Tex, he would drop in and see her before he hit south.

With nightfall, the Texan headed toward Hanging Wells. When the lights of town glowed through the velvety darkness like clustered fireflies, he pulled off the trail and worked around them. A full moon flooded the flats and he had little difficulty in locating the O'Keefe place.

Warily, he approached from the rear, bumped a barbed wire fence. Tex looped his reins around a fence post and squirmed under the wire. A few hundred yards ahead, the windows of the house were bright with light. Cautiously he eased toward the square outline of the building.

The rapid clip-clop of fast-trotting ponies, steadily drawing closer, reached his ears. A posse? In quick alarm Tex hunted cover. A small barn bulked at the rear of the house. Mentally cursing the moonlight, he ran toward it and threw himself at full length in its welcome shadow.

Plain to his straining eyes, three riders rounded the house. One led a spare pony, saddled and bridled. Two drew rein, while the third walked his mount to the back door and whistled.

A girl threw open the door. The lamplight, streaming from within, glinted upon her coppery hair.

"Oh, Tim!" There was indescribable joy in Kathryn O'Keefe's greeting. The rider swung out of the saddle. His features were plain to the dumb-

founded Texan—a square-faced freckled rider with
heavy jaw. He wore a ten-gallon hat, silk shirt and
twin guns. Silver conchas studded his gun-belt. Tex
knew the type and disgust welled within him. These
were border desperadoes. The breed frequented
Mexican dives by the dozen, terrorized greenhorns
and specialized in bushwhacking. "Jest the brand
of coyote a gal would fall for!" the stricken man
muttered, as Kathryn threw her arms around the
newcomer's neck and he impatiently allowed her to
kiss him.

For a while, the two, standing close, conversed
in low tones. Then, with another ardent embrace,
the girl called out a wistful "Adios!" and stepped
into the house. The stranger mounted his pony, rejoined his companions, and the three jogged toward town.

Something died within Tex. Until those paralyz-
ing moments when he saw Kathryn O'Keefe in the
arms of a stranger he had never realized the depth
of the feeling he had for the spunky saloon man's
daughter. Lying at full length, hooked fingers dig-
ging into the ground, he sipped his fill of the cup of
bitterness. It was as though the last strong rope to
which he had clung had proved faulty, snapped
and plunged him into a black abyss of despair.

Wearily he dragged to his feet and plodded back
to the buckskin. Slumped in the saddle, he heeled
the pony to a gallop and rode recklessly toward
town. In his present mood the Texan cared little for
a possible posse and less for his life.

Silhouetted against the skyline ahead, three
riders bobbed into view. Tex pulled his racing pony
down, eyes contracted. These were Kathryn's vis-

itors. What was their business anyway? And why a led pony? His gloom dissolving in the scent of trouble, he stuck to their trail.

On the outskirts of town, the trio slanted off, heading for the residential section. With mounting curiosity, the Texan lazed behind. Understanding flowed into his mind as they jogged past darkened homes, toward Doc Hoskins's hospital.

A lamp burned in the surgery. Tex glimpsed the doctor, carefully dripping a liquid from a bottle into a spoon. The three riders circled the house and cautiously approached an open window in the darkened hospital.

Sitting his pony in the shadow of a cottonwood, the Texan watched one man dismount and wriggle through the window. In a few moments, Moreland's bandaged hand thrust into view as the rider pushed him from within. Another rider dismounted and helped lever the helpless foreman's bulky body through the window frame.

Swiftly and silently, they worked the injured man outside and boosted him onto the led pony. Then, with Moreland setting the pace, they hit westward, at a jingling trot.

Behind them rode the Texan. All else was forgotten save that his big chance had come. The four men ahead were members of the payroll gang, and they were leading him to the long-sought renegade hideout.

Before the night was over Tex was thankful for the full moon. It lit mesquite flats and valley swales with white splendor, against which the four black dots far ahead were plain to the lone tracker. When

the terrain swelled into hills and finally broke up
into the rocky chaos of the Barrens, he edged
closer, reckless of discovery in his eagerness to trail
the wolves to their den.

The early morning hours found Tex still dogging
the renegades, picking his way through a medley of
canyons and ravines, ever seeking the shadows as
he drifted in the wake of the four riders bunched a
scant mile ahead. Finally, they dropped into a wide
shallow basin, dotted with solitary buttes and
headed toward what was apparently an unbroken
escarpment that walled the basin on the further
side.

Fearful of discovery in the open, Tex dropped
back, his eyes following the progress of his quarry
until they were enveloped by the shadow of the
nearest butte. When they again emerged into the
moonlight, he rode forward at an angle, to screen
himself from observation by the bulk of the butte.

The rock wall loomed close, but still the renegades bored steadily ahead. Tex sought the welcome cover of a second butte, rounded its eroding
flank on the shadowed side and searched ahead for
the riders . . . but they had disappeared as completely as though the earth had opened and swallowed
them. Throwing caution to the wind, he rode out
into the light-flooded open. Solid and forbidding,
the great wall quickly brought him up short.
Bewildered, he wheeled and eyed the basin, empty
save for the great flat-topped buttes, standing like
mighty sentinels.

"Ef that don't beat all creation!" he told the
buckskin. "Either them hombres sprouted wings
like angels, or I'm locoed."

For a mile he rode along the base of the wall, his pony's hooves sinking deep into heaped talus, hunting for a break in the rock—in vain. He doubled back, bent low in the saddle, seeking tracks of the disappearing horsemen, but for long stretches wind and storm had swept the dust away and an army could have marched over the bare rock without leaving sign.

Finally, in angry perplexity, Tex headed for the base of the nearest butte and bedded down, determined to resume his search at dawn.

The rising sun painted the far-flung beetling rock wall with ever-changing shades of peach, pink and saffron, glowing symphonies of color that scintillated in glorious harmony, until erased by ever-mounting waves of white light. Tex toiled up the precipitous slope of the butte, hand over hand, working from ledge to ledge. Its lofty summit towered high above the wall and he was curious to learn what lay beyond.

Sweated and scratched, fingers raw, he breasted the rim and hauled his aching body onto the top, which lay flat as a billiard table. Picking a path through the rocky debris, he approached its west side, overlooking the wall, dropped low and snaked forward.

A low whistle of amazement left his lips as he eyed the scene outspread below. At his feet was the wall shrunk to pigmy size. Behind it, the arid terrain rose in a succession of benches to stark heights, towering in a gigantic backdrop of tortured rock. But his eager gaze focused upon a cuplike depression, verdant green, so close that it seemed he could have dropped a rock upon it. It appeared to be completely hemmed in by precipitous cliffs, but the searcher's glasses detected a crack in the rock wall—the door through which Moreland and his three cohorts had slipped the night before.

The hidden box canyon was almost circular. In the chaparral Tex sighted the roofs of several adobes. Black ant-like dots that were men moved around. A tenuous finger of smoke curled upward from a fire, to slowly dissolve in the clear air. This, then, was the hideaway of the payroll gang!

Exulting, the Texan reviewed the possibilities of his discovery. In twelve hours he could rush a posse from Hanging Wells and bottle up the renegades. With care, he again searched the canyon sides with his glasses, seeking sign of another exit, but there was none. His pulse raced with suppressed excitement. As if to atone for the knockout blow that had smashed his hopes in the sheriff's office, fate had handed him a royal flush in the shape of this opportunity to clear his name and round up the worst gang of desperadoes that had terrorized Concha County in years.

He wriggled back from the edge of the butte, straightened, and hurried to the further side.

Descent proved more difficult than the upward climb. Clinging to the rough, outjutting rock, fumbling with his sharp-toed riding boots for footholds, he lowered himself foot by foot, until finally, with a gasp of relief, he dropped onto a yielding pile of powdered talus at the butte's base.

He hastened toward the buckskin, drowsing in a nest of cluttered boulders. Snatching his spurs off the horn, he bent to strap them on, when a rasping challenge grated on his ears, "Stretch, mister!"

Slowly the Texan straightened, crooked fingers poised over his gun butt. His gun hand dropped away as he faced the gaping muzzles of three six-guns, backed by three pairs of bleak eyes. No need to ask who they were, he thought bitterly, as he eyed the soiled silk shirts, widespread sombreros and dark, pocked features of the two who faced him—Moreland's renegades. Too late, he cursed his carelessness. He had been sighted on the night ride and the Box-C foreman had neatly trapped him.

He raised his arms and turned his head slightly to take in the third man—it was Kansas, the deadliest gunman of the Scarface gang. There was no recognition in the killer's pale eyes. Tex remembered his threat, "Ef I had a gun I'd gutshoot yuh." Coiled rope in his hand, Kansas slithered forward and lifted the captive's gun out of leather. "Drop yuh wings!" he rasped. As Tex's arms came down the gunman slipped a loop over each wrist, jerked it tight and wrenched the prisoner's arms together behind his back.

Securely trussed, the Texan was pushed into his saddle. Kansas led the buckskin, while his two companions rode behind.

It was small consolation to the chagrined Texan to discover that his surmise was correct. A split in the rock wall, which he had ridden past without observing the previous night, gave access to the box canyon. It was so narrow that his stirrups almost scraped on either side. In single file, the party threaded through, to emerge in a rock-girded bowl, thick with chaparral.

The renegades wound through the brush and reined up at a crude adobe. At their hail, Monte Moreland, right arm strapped to his chest, left hand heavily bandaged, strode out. His dark features creased in a malicious grin as he eyed the trussed Texan.

"You poked thet long snout of yours inter my affairs once too often," he growled. "This time I stop yore clock f'r keeps. Tie him up!"

Two of the renegades hauled Tex off his pony, dragged him to a nearby piñon, and lashed him to the trunk. Helpless, only his head free, he awaited his fate.

The hours dragged by, but no further attention was paid the prisoner. Twenty paces distant stood Moreland's adobe. Men entered and left continually, but the Box-C foreman remained inside. Tex's hat had toppled off his head and the sun, arcing overhead, beat down through the sparse shade. An olla of water stood on a bench by the adobe, to torture his eyes. Beneath the bench stood a number of small barrels and a coil of fuse. Gunpowder, he thought. What deviltry had Moreland in mind?

At last the craving for water grew unbearable. In response to his hoarse shouts, the foreman stepped out of the adobe, strolled over and eyed his prisoner.

"Gimme a drink!" gasped the Texan.

"Why waste good water on a measly nester?" inquired Moreland affably. "You won't be thirsty—long." He reached for the makin's, then remembered that his left arm was useless. Features contorted with passion, he waved the bandaged hand before his prisoner's face, snarled, "You blasted bustard, yo're payin' f'r this." Then his mood changed. Again his voice became deep and smooth. "Mebbe we'll pull out tomorrow, then I'll leave you one of them, with a lighted fuse." He chuckled and nodded toward the barrels.

"Thet's black powder," he continued. "Next time we'll grab the gold afore it reaches town—derail the train. Pity you won't be there t' see it!"

CHAPTER 19

Burned and blinded by the fiery sun, wrists raw with fruitless straining against the tight-lashed rope, throat parched and thickened tongue lolling from between cracked lips, the Texan hung, half conscious, against his bonds.

Weighted with suffering, the hours dragged.

Night, and a cooling breeze, brought merciful respite. The prisoner raised his head and filled his lungs with the keen air. Darkness walled him, save for a rectangle of white that marked the entrance to Moreland's adobe. Overhead, the stars, like a multitude of shimmering diamonds bedecking the robes of the gods, shone in cold beauty.

Eyes aching from the sun-glare, Tex watched the sky. Might as well get a good look, he thought whimsically, and make the most of it. If the renegades didn't pull out before the sun set again and leave a powder barrel with a spluttering fuse behind, he'd be crazy after another day's exposure to the sun, without food or water.

Moreland's light blinked out and the deep silence of the solitudes enveloped the basin. A night hawk chittered shrill overhead, a pony whinnied, but no other sound disturbed the serenity of the night. Gradually the prisoner's chin dropped onto his chest and he drifted into uneasy sleep.

Years on the range had sharpened the Texan's perceptions until they approached the keenness of an animal's. Of a sudden he was wide awake, head up, staring into the dark.

A white band of light on the cliffs across the basin marked the rising moon. Nothing else had changed since he dropped into a doze, yet something had awakened him.

Ears keened, he listened.

Behind him, and out of his range of vision, a dry twig snapped. It might have been a night animal on the prowl, but the prisoner tensed.

The taut rawhide rope that lashed his body twanged. He heard the soft sawing of a knife. Before his astonished eyes the rope dropped away. The thongs that bound his legs and wrists soon followed.

Free, he swayed on numb legs, in which circulation had long since died, and flopped helplessly to the ground.

Amazement surged through the Texan's mind as he vigorously rubbed his deadened limbs until the blood commenced to flow and prickle as though myriad cholla thorns lacerated the flesh.

He staggered to his feet and balanced gingerly, then became aware that a spare figure—blurred in the gloom—was standing silently by the tree trunk.

Kansas's cold voice—pitched low—rasped through the dark. "Reckon thet evens us up."

Enlightenment flooded Tex's mind. This was the snake-eyed gunman's gesture of thanks, or more likely a salve to his injured pride, for release from jail when the Scarface gang was smashed.

"I'm thankin' yuh." The Texan's voice was hoarse and cracked. "Figgered I was due f'r the Pearly Gates."

"Yuh don't have t' butter me," snarled the killer. "Next time I'm comin' a-shootin'. Yore hoss's tied at the wall." Without further words, he turned and faded into the night as silently as he had appeared.

Tex's first move was to cat-toe to the olla, dip cup after cup of the precious fluid and quench the long-drawn torture of his thirst. From inside the adobe resounded Moreland's gurgling snore.

The Texan softly replaced the cup on the bench and stood irresolute, battling a consuming impulse to steal inside and throttle the sleeping renegade. Moreland was helpless. He could choke the life out of the dark-skinned foreman and steal away unseen. Fingers crooked, the released prisoner quivered with bitter resentment as he thought of the day's torture beneath the sun. Then he relaxed, the craving for vengeance subdued by another idea.

Carefully he rolled a powder barrel from beneath the bench and picked up the coil of fuse. Shouldering the barrel, and alert for a possible lookout, he followed the winding trail through the brush toward the canyon mouth.

Something moved in the shadow of the cliff wall. The fugitive dropped the barrel and threw himself flat. Cuddling the ground, he slowly snaked forward, rose to his feet with a quick release of breath when he distinguished the buckskin, tied to a squat mesquite. Kansas had not lied.

He led his pony through the slot, returned and again hoisted the barrel to his shoulder. Midway through the narrow passage he dumped his load, pried off a stave with the stout blade of his Barlow knife and set the barrel on end. It was pitch dark, but he could feel the soft caress of the fine powder as it spilled through the gap. Next he unwound the length of fuse, inserted one end deep within the barrel and carefully strung it toward the further end of the slot. On his knees, he fingered the fuse back to the barrel. Satisfied, the Texan, from force of habit, reached up to pluck a match from his hatband, then abruptly realized that he had no hat. He searched his vest pockets, pants pockets, in vain, and despair iced his veins. Then he hastened to his pony and frantically turned out the saddle bags. His eager fingers fastened on a bundle of "stinker" matches, sealed with tallow, in an empty cartridge case. At a run he returned to the slot, groped for the end of the fuse, ignited it.

Triumph in his eyes, he watched the spluttering fire creep over the ground, like a great sparkling, scarlet insect, then headed for his pony and leaped into leather. Kneeing the animal to a gallop, he rode out into the basin.

A quarter mile distant Tex pulled the buckskin down, whirled and waited. Nothing happened. Once again he suffered the pangs of frustration as the seconds crept by. Was the fuse defective? Had some skulking renegade sighted him and extinguished the spark? Maybe the Kansan, having paid his debt, had dogged him and guessed his purpose? These and a dozen other questions whirled through his mind.

All doubts were dispelled by a red flash and an ear-splitting detonation that reverberated away through the canyons like thunder. Crowding it, a succession of crashes, as rock poured down from the heights into the slot, beat upon his ears. Slowly the cataclysm subsided, the echoes rumbled into distance and again quiet enshrouded the basin.

Tex rode toward the wall through a fog of choking dust.

The slot was jammed with sundered rock as high as his exulting eyes could see through the dust pall. A huge pile of debris marked the entrance. The renegades were trapped.

A smile of pure delight wreathed the Texan's sun-scorched features. Wheeling, he headed across the silent basin, hell-bent for Hanging Wells.

As the clatter of the buckskin's hooves died in the distance, a bearded figure emerged out from the shadow of the nearest butte on a bony mule and ambled toward the wall.

In the gray dawn, a hatless rider urged his jaded pony between the deserted hitch racks of the county seat. At the picket fence of Sheriff Cummings's frame dwelling, he slid painfully out of leather and walked stiff-legged to the door.

Nightshirt hastily stuffed into his pants, the sheriff eased the door open and peered out in response to his insistent banging.

"F'r gosh sakes!" growled the lawman, blinking at Tex's stubbled, fatigue-lined features. "I figgered you was on the wrong side of the border."

"I got the payroll bunch corraled," shot back the Texan. "We gotta git a posse out t' the Barrens, pronto, afore the rats gnaw a hole in the trap." Quickly he told of his misadventures and final escape.

"Dawgone it, Tex, ef you ain't a jewel," ejaculated the lawman. "Step inside and rest yore laigs while I git my harness on. Ma!" he yelled.

"Stir up some chow and brew some cawfee. We gotta ramble."

An hours later a dozen horsemen loped out of Hanging Wells. Astride a fresh pony, Tex sided the sheriff. Through the growing light they drummed over the silvered flats.

"Dan," burst out the Texan abruptly, "I thought you were a pard."

"Wal, ain't I?" countered the old sheriff, swaying easily in the saddle.

"You shore don't act thet way," grumbled Tex. "I brought in Moreland, plunked his cut of the payroll loot right on yore desk, and then like a jughead you swaller a passel of lies. Dammit, you said he was a renegade yourself. Then you take Cresswell's side and thet smooth-tongue banker. And you can't shoot worth a damn!"

The sheriff chuckled throatily at the final crowning insult. Ahead, a jack-rabbit popped up, shook his stubby tail and shot away through the brush with quick bounding jumps. Cummings palmed his six-gun, threw down on the elusive, fast-disappearing animal. The gun roared and the mangled remains of the jack-rabbit twisted in mid-air.

Tex watched with wide open eyes. "How come yuh missed me from the courthouse steps?" he demanded.

"I ain't loco enough t' plug the slickest deputy I ever stuck a badge on," grunted Cummings. "All but one," he amended. "You got a lot t' learn, Tex, and the first is thet things ain't always what they seem. When yo're settin' in a stud game, it's the hole card thet counts and yuh kin do a hell of a lot of bluffin'. You ain't seen my hole card yet. Trou-

ble with young bucks like you is, you flash yore
hands too damned quick."

Thereafter, Tex was silent, pondering on the old
lawman's words.

The sun was high when they hit the basin. At the
pile of debris that blocked the cut, they brought
their horses to a halt.

Cummings eyed the choked passage. "A jasper
could scramble over thet," he commented.

"Meanin' that ef we kin git in, they kin git out,"
said Tex.

"You get the idea, but I gamble they went out
afoot."

"Le's go see!" suggested the Texan, dismounting.

With three agile punchers, he scrambled up the
heaped rock. It was easy climbing. The four
worked their way over the top and looked down
into the verdant quietude of the canyon. Nothing
stirred, save the quail in the long grass.

The possemen worked their way down on the
other side and filed through the chaparral, alert for
trouble. But Moreland's adobe was deserted.
Blankets were heaped in a corner and bottles littered a rough table. Two other adobes, deeper in
the brush, showed signs of hasty departure.
Clothing and oddments of saddlery were scattered
around. The cook shack was fully stocked and the
ground beneath the dead embers of the campfire
was warm.

In a pole corral, a bunch of ponies milled
around.

"Finest hoss-flesh I ever set eyes on," declared a
puncher, with longing eyes.

But a thorough search of the little basin uncovered not a single human being. The vultures had flown.

Tex let down the corral bars and released the ponies. They were destined to spend the rest of their lives in the canyon, but, as he pointed out to his companions, there was grass and water aplenty. Then the four men clambered over the blocked entrance and rejoined the rest of the possemen.

Tex shook his head glumly in response to the sheriff's inquiring glance. Once again the payroll gang had eluded the law.

CHAPTER 20

"Wal, they're hoofin' it," commented Cummings. The veteran sheriff's eyes swept the boulder-studded basin. "I'd shore hate t' be set afoot in this particular corner of hell."

"The ashes of their fire ain't cold yet." Tex frowned at the long seamed stretch of the wall. "I'll gamble the sidewinders have gone t' earth here-abouts."

"Quit settin' around like a flock of broody hens," snapped the sheriff, glaring at the lounging possemen. "Scatter, get busy and hunt sign."

The riders hit leather, fanned out and circled, bent low in the saddle.

Tex rode northward along the base of the wall. For a few hundred yards the buckskin's hooves rang on rock, then sank into wind-drifted patches of piled talus. The Texan ground-hitched the pony and, afoot, cast around like a hound on the scent. His excited shout brought the possemen at a gallop. They peeled out of their saddles and bunched around his bent figure, eyeing footsteps, plainly marked in the yielding dust.

"Reckon a dozen hombres legged it," he announced, moving toward his pony. "Let's go!"

"Hold yuhr hosses!" grunted the old sheriff,

squinting at the plainly marked trail through the dust drift. His eyes sought the impatient Tex, foot in the stirrup. "You acquainted with Monte Moreland?" he asked.

Tex snorted, "I got doggone good reason to know the bustard."

"He's quarter Apache," drawled Cummings. "Know what thet spells?"

"Cunnin' as a coyote," rapped the Texan.

"Yet he trails his gang through a dust drift, makin' plain sign when there's a full moon and bare rock all around." The sheriff's faded eyes held an amused gleam. "Trouble with you young bucks is thet you take the bit in yore teeth and split the breeze like crazy colts. We're ridin' south."

For a moment Tex's eyes clouded at the reproof, then he grinned. "Takes an old mosshorn like you t' figger it out. You lead, Dan!"

The posse cantered southward. The wall, an impassable barrier, sprawled on their right. To the left swept the wide reach of the basin, sprinkled with towering buttes. Ahead rose range after range of rugged mountains, bleak and brownish-yellow in the searing heat, cradled in a hopeless tangle of waterless gulches and canyons.

A dot danced on the heat waves afar off.

"Ain't that somebody on a hoss?" queried Tex, staring through slitted eyes.

"On a mule!" grunted Cheyenne, a half-breed puncher.

Slowly the dot took shape, grew larger, materialized into the Preacher, jogging peacefully toward them on his mule.

"Ef I don't meet up with that hairpin in the unlikeliest places," muttered Tex.

As he drew close, the bearded Preacher raised his arm in greeting, reined up as the possemen clustered around. His piercing dark eyes surveyed the dust-coated men and ponies.

"Man is born to trouble, as the sparks fly upward," he intoned. "Are you on the trail of an evildoer?"

"A passel of doggoned evildoers," grunted the sheriff. "The payroll gang is hoofin' it hereabouts. Mebbe you sighted the galoots?"

Paul stroked his flowing black beard. "Would they be headed by one Moreland of the Box-C, whose arms are bandaged?"

"You said it!" ejaculated Tex, eyes eager. "Spill the beans, Preacher, f'r gosh sakes."

"I could lead you to them," returned Paul placidly. "but why travel in the heat of the day?" he gazed longingly toward the shadow of an overhanging butte. "Let us tarry awhile! The Lord said, 'Rest ye who are weary.' "

"Let's git goin', Preacher," burst out Tex, nerves frazzled by long hours in the saddle. "These bustards are as slippery as rattlesnakes."

"Headstrong as a mustang," commented the sheriff dryly. He wheeled toward the shade. "Let's rest our saddles awhile."

Inwardly raging, Tex tailed him and the ambling mule.

Nothing loath to shelter from the burning heat of midday, the possemen loosened girths, rocked their saddles and hunkered against the base of the butte.

Paul produced a sack of tobacco and papers from the tail of his shiny frock coat and gravely rolled a smoke.

"Don't the Lord frown on tobacco and such like?" inquired Tex acidly, still rankled by the delay.

"The Good Book says, 'There went up smoke out of his nostrils,' " returned Paul blandly. "Therefore, my son, it is not offensive in the sight of the Lord."

He inhaled luxuriously and addressed the sheriff. "In the hour before dawn these men passed the spot where I lay asleep and aroused me with their foul language, which," his eyes fell full upon Tex, "is not seemly to the Lord. Amazed to find men afoot in the Barrens, I followed these footsore men. They are now resting in a draw some four miles along the wall."

"Then what are we waitin' for?" demanded Tex, rising to his feet.

The Preacher sighed. "The impetuosity of youth! I am a man of peace, but I observed that these malefactors were armed. Why approach in daylight and be greeted by lead? Why not steal up upon them with the darkness and overcome them with ease?"

Tex eyed the strong face of the Preacher narrowly. He had not forgotten Paul's unexpected presence when Markham, the bank clerk, was murdered, and his eagerness to learn if the renegades' accomplice had talked. Nor had he forgotten the Preacher's marksmanship. Was it mere chance that he should be wandering in the Barrens? Was he tolling the posse away while Moreland and his gang made a getaway?

"You shore got plenty of fight savvy—f'r a preacher," he commented caustically. He swung around to the sheriff, comfortably stretched out by

Paul's side. "Let's mosey along!"

"We'll stick around here 'til sundown, like the Preacher says," Cummings said. "Then, I reckon, he'll set us on the right trail."

"Ef we lose em—" began Tex heatedly.

"Button up!" yawned the sheriff. He jerked his Stetson down over his eyes. "I'm gonna take a siesta."

With night, a shadowy bunch of riders drifted southward behind Paul's slow-pacing mule. Dim to their right, the barricade of the wall was broken, pierced by ravines and twisting canyons. Into one the Preacher wheeled, stopped and stepped off his animal.

Around him, the possemen hit the dirt.

Paul's deep voice boomed in the gloom. "The men you seek are in the next canyon. As a man of peace, I will remain and watch your ponies."

"Suits me," rejoined Cummings. "Unstrap them spurs, you saddle stiffs, and foller me." He moved off, the possemen stringing behind.

Tex edged forward, shouldered the sheriff. "Gosh darn it, Dan!" His voice was strained with urgency. "Don't leave that man unguarded. Mebbe he'll 'cross us and run the ponies off. They's something mighty queer about that guy."

"Quit belly-achin' and stick close," growled Cummings. "Paul's no double-crosser." His voice rose. "Close up, you ranakins!"

In the dim starlight, the group of possemen moved out of the ravine and followed the sheriff's spare form, awkward in high-heeled boots.

Two hundred paces along the wall, another canyon gaped black. Cummings held up a restraining hand, silently eased ahead, Tex at his heels.

The pair rounded a shoulder of the rock—and froze in their tracks. Midway down the canyon a fire blazed, its flickering flames reflected on the polished walls that frowned high on either side. Dark-featured men hunkered around the fire. Tex caught a glimpse of Moreland's soiled bandages.

Slowly the sheriff backed, Tex beside him, until they were out of the renegades' line of vision. Then Cummings waved his possemen forward. Unhurriedly the sheriff gave his order.

"Hist 'em!" The brisk challenge rapped out of the darkness and cut through the rumble of talk around the fire as though with a sharp knife.

Incredulous silence draped the dark-visaged renegades. Heads pivoted as they stared in the direction of the sound. Some raised faltering arms. One wiry outlaw, with pale eyes, stabbed for his twin guns. From the night three irons barked, arousing the echoes, and Kansas flopped lifeless into the leaping flames. Another renegade ducked and plunged for the sheltering darkness, dodging like a scared rabbit. Again hidden guns spurted death and he pitched headlong.

Arms jerked skyward, the remaining bandits crowded together like a herd of spooked steers, uneasy eyes searching for their unseen assailants.

The firelight glinted on Sheriff Cummings' star as he stepped forward, six-gun leveled.

"Line up!" he barked, "and no shenanigans."

Ten men shuffled into line, the bandaged Moreland among them. Possemen closed in from either side. Two worked down the dazed row of desperadoes, slipping guns out of holsters and knives out of sheaths.

Tex's glowering eyes fastened, not on Moreland, but on the square, devil-may-care features of the man Kathryn called Tim. "Ef only he had made a break!" he thought bitterly. Unconsciously his fingers slipped over the smooth butt of his gun and he glanced down at the scorched remains of Kansas.

"Two of you hairpins rustle the cavvy," directed Cummings. "Reckon we kin snatch a mite of shuteye afore we hit f'r town."

Tex and Cheyenne headed for the mouth of the canyon.

Ground-hitched, the ponies were bunched where the possemen had peeled out of leather, but the cavvyman—the Preacher—and his mule had disappeared.

"Reckon gunfire scared the bible-puncher," commented Cheyenne, as they gathered the hanging reins.

"Like hell it did," grunted Tex, eyes puzzled. "You ain't seen him in action. Paul's worse'n a wildcat when he goes on the rampage, but I shore ain't got him figered out."

Loiterers on the plankwalks of Hanging Wells gazed open-mouthed when an unshaven, blaspheming bunch of renegades straggled painfully into town, herded by bored possemen. Sheriff Cummings, sardonic humor sparkling in his deep-set eyes, had decreed that they should hoof every foot from the Barrens to the county seat. One beady-eyed desperado refused to budge, but Cummings changed his ideas by the simple expedient of dabbing a loop around his thick neck and leaving. When they eased the taut rope and the objector choked back to life, throat dull red from the rope weal, he walked—gladly.

The prisoners were hustled into the hoosegow and Tex, despondent and bone-weary, sank into a chair in the sheriff's office. For a while he gloomed in silence, then Cummings jingled in, followed by the heavy-jawed renegade they called Tim.

Bristling like a terrier at sight of trouble, the Texan jumped to his feet and stood stiff-legged.

"Turnin' state's evidence and savin' yore lousy hide?" he mocked.

"Why not?" grinned the renegade cheerfully. "I don't crave no harp."

"Quit funnin', Tim," snapped the sheriff. He turned to Tex. "Meet Tim O'Keefe, best deputy I ever pinned a badge on."

"O'Keefe!" gulped Tex.

"Shore," grinned the freckled rider. "Kath's brother. Reckon yo're the Texan she's so crazy about."

Tex's jaw dropped. Then he gathered his bemused senses and a glad light glowed in his tired eyes. He stepped close to the stocky Tim. It dawned on him that the young rider was a mighty good-looking hombre, the kind of guy who'd head into hell with a cheerful grin, and he'd been yearning to salivate the hairpin!

"How in heck come you—" he stammered, but Cummings broke in, slammed a bottle on the desk.

"Wet your whistles, boys!" he invited. "You done a good job, both of yuh." He tilted the bottle, then slid down contentedly into his swivel chair and eyed Tex. "Told yuh I had an ace in the hole— this is it. Tim rode f'r the Box-C. I figgered

Moreland was hittin' a crooked trail so I deputized
Tim and told him t' keep cases on Moreland. Wal,
he hit up Monte f'r dinero, constant. Seems like he
was always flat broke. Monte promised t' show
him how to make some easy money—which he did.
Thet was after you drifted inter town, Tex. He's got
enough on Moreland and the gang t' swing the
bustard. You turned out trumps, Tim!"

The freckle-faced rider took another swig of the
sheriff's good bourbon. "I ain't got em all, Dan,"
he objected. "Never could locate the king-pin."

"Mebbe there just ain't no king-pin," suggested
Tex.

High-pitched expostulations, the shuffle of feet
and Preacher Paul's deep voice resounded in the
corridor outside. The door flew open and a disheveled, indignant Heinemann, squirming in the grasp
of the Preacher's brawny hand, was thrust into the
room.

"Friend," he admonished the struggling banker,
"I do thee no wrong." With ease he propelled the
protesting man toward a chair, dumped him into it
like a sack of feed. "The Lord said, Deliver us from
evil.' As his humble servant I but deliver you into
the hands of justice."

Heinemann squirmed to his feet, features contorted, mouthed incoherent protests, but the
massive Preacher shook him into silence as a terrier
shakes a rat.

Paul addressed the sheriff. "My friend, it was the
Lord's wish that I led you to the renegades. Now I
bring you their leader. There is deceit on his lips
and murder in his mind. If you will ride to the Box-
C, peer into the old well behind the horse barn, you
will find his ill-gotten store of gold. Alas that such

a whited sepulcher should deceive the people!"

With a final shake that caused the pallid Heinemann to totter, he boomed, "Though their sins be as scarlet they shall be white as snow."

Cummings rose, a triumphant glint in his eyes, and lifted the jail keys off a peg. "You shore had me hog-swiggled," he admitted, grabbing the shrinking banker's shoulder. "Now we got a full hand—ace high."

Heinemann's almost hysterical protests died away down the corridor.

CHAPTER 21

The Preacher stalked from the office in the wake of Cummings and his prisoner. "There are souls to be saved," he announced sonorously. "The Lord calls and I must go."

Cummings returned and flung his keys on the desk.

"Ain't thet preacher a fox?" he ejaculated. "Who in hell woulda figgered Heinemann f'r the king-pin? Now we corraled the whole shebang, le's ride t' the Box-C and gather up the gold."

It was night when the three men rode into Cresswell's spread. The squeaking of a fiddle and roar of voices as the cowhands joined in lusty chorus flowed from the bunkhouse. In contrast, the ranch house stood dark and silent.

Cresswell thumped out upon the porch in answer to the sheriff's hail.

"Moreland's in the jug and the whole danged payroll gang," shouted Cummings. "The loot's cached in yore well, behind the barn. We're gonna search!"

The cowman leaned wearily on the porch rail. He seemed to sag. All the life had seeped out of him, as though the fires of belligerency that had blazed so fiercely through the years had burned out, leaving the dead husk of a man.

"Search all yuh damn please," he rumbled. "My gal's quit me and took the train east. Now Monte's 'crossed the spread. Reckon I'm jest about through."

"I'm takin' up my homestead again," challenged Tex, "and ef yore saddle pounders butt in I'll round up every nester in fifty miles and burn this joint down."

The old man turned faded eyes upon the sharp-voiced Texan. "The valley is open—wide open. Now my gal's gone I got no one t' fight for." A little of the old fire fused his voice. "And damn you f'r a blasted nester!"

Slowly straightening, he turned and moved ponderously into the darkened house.

Cummings wheeled and led the way to the rear of the big horse barn. Dismounting, he bent over the decaying planking that covered the long disused well. Eagerly the three men threw the planks to one side and stared down into the gaping hole.

"Whar in hell—" muttered the sheriff. Then his hand, exploring the rim of the well, came up grasping a bulky, black-bound book.

"Paul's Bible!" exclaimed Tex.

Cummings threw the book down and a white sheet of paper slipped from between the pages. Tex struck a match, twisted a handful of straw together and ignited it. But nothing lay before them save a dry hole in the ground, surrounded by moldering timbers.

Idly Tex picked up the white sheet that protruded from the Bible's pages. He read a scrawled inscription aloud, "See Romans 16:18.—Adios, Paul."

"This ain't a Bible meetin'," barked Cummings.
"We're huntin' gold."

Former suspicions blazed in the Texan's mind.
Wordlessly, by the light of the makeshift torch held
high by Tim, he thumbed through the Bible's un-
familiar pages until he hit the sixteenth chapter of
Romans, verse 18. Aloud he read:

"For they that are such serve not the Lord Jesus
Christ, but their own belly; and by good words
and fair speeches deceive the hearts of the
simple."

"Now tell me how in thunder thet helps us," demanded Cummings.

"I got a sneakin' hunch thet friend Paul run a
sandy over us," returned Tex slowly. "What d'ye
know about that guy?"

"Nothing," snapped Cummings, "except he
flashed a U. S. marshal's badge on me once. Said t'
dumb up."

A thought struck Tex. This was the last day of
the month.

"Payroll come in?"

"Smornin'. It's cached in the bank."

"I gamble thet's why he wanted Heinemann out
of the way," muttered Tex, reluctant admiration in
his voice. "He tolled us out here t' git the run of the
bank and grab a good four hours' start. I'll stake
my saddle he's helling f'r the border right now."

"Yo're loco!" The fuming sheriff irritably
pitched a rock into the well and listened to the faint
splash far below.

"I wager Paul was the king-pin," persisted Tex.
"And is he slick, the rattlesnake! He double-
crossed his gang, grabbed their cut of the loot.

Busted into the bank, lifted another payroll and vamoosed."

"Quit runnin' off at the mouth." Cummings's voice was brusque, but there was no conviction in his uneasy tone.

"Le's go see!" returned Tex laconically, mounting his buckskin.

The three pulled up hard-breathing ponies outside the bank and hurried into the darkened entrance. At Tex's kick, the door swung open . . . they surged across the polished floor and rounded the counter. The massive safe gaped open. A quick inspection revealed that it was empty, save for neatly stacked packs of documents.

Cummings hot-footed for his office, grabbed the jail keys and rushed downstairs, to reappear quickly with the angrily expostulating banker. "It's a trick," spluttered Heinemann, "to steal the payroll. Watch the bank, or is it too late?" Sobered by sudden apprehension, he eyed the glum-faced lawmen.

"The Preacher lifted the dinero," growled Cummings, for once abashed.

"You fuddle-brained fools!" yelled Heinemann. "I'll—" His agonized voice rang upon Tex's ears as he ducked out and hurried down the corridor. He had more important business on hand than to stand and be blasted by the unfortunate banker's just wrath.

Swinging into leather, he hit for the O'Keefe place. Lights glowed bright at the windows as he rounded the house. Dismounting, he tapped on the back door and whistled softly.

The door swung open and Kathryn stood in the stream of light.

"Why, Tex!" There was incredulous delight in

her astonished cry. "I thought you were—miles away."

"I ain't on the dodge no more," Tex grinned like a schoolboy. "I'm hittin' f'r the valley. Gonna build another cabin on my homestead and run a few steers. Say, I got the prettiest little place down at Indian Bluff."

"Yes!" Her voice was flat.

"It's kinda lonely f'r a man alone," mused the Texan, "nothin' but coyotes out there."

Kathryn edged closer. "I'm not scared of coyotes, and I can cook and bake and keep house."

"It's rough, homesteadin'," he grunted, "and I ain't got much dinero."

"Does it matter?" she whispered.

Then his arms enfolded her.

In the sheriff's office gaunt old Dan Cummings thumbed through a stack of yellowed reward notices. Frequently he paused, eyed the blurred picture of a wanted man, then searched on. Finally he held up a sheet, brown with age, and squinted at the features of a clean-shaven individual with high forehead and piercing eyes. Slowly he read:

$5,000 REWARD
Wanted for Bank Robbery

Samuel Larson, alias Scripture Sam. Height 6 feet 2 inches, weight 220. Black hair, hook nose. Wanted for robbery with violence. Held up Winchester County Bank, Culver City Bank and National Bank of Pueblo. Escaped from Stillwater jail. Dangerous character, fast with gun, well educated, was trained for Holy Orders. Usually operates alone.

Slowly, with his pencil, the sheriff sketched a beard on Larson's square jaw—it was Preacher Paul to the life!

There are a lot more
where this one came from!

Winners of the SPUR and WESTERN HERITAGE AWARD

08383	**The Buffalo Runners** Fred Grove	$1.75
13905	**The Day The Cowboys Quit** Elmer Kelton	$1.25
29741	**Gold In California** Todhunter Ballard	$1.25
34270	**The Honyocker** Giles Lutz	$1.50
47082	**The Last Days of Wolf Garnett** Clifton Adams	$1.75
47491	**Law Man** Lee Leighton	$1.50
55123	**My Brother John** Herbert Purdum	$1.75
56025	**The Nameless Breed** Will C. Brown	$1.50
71153	**The Red Sabbath** Lewis B. Patten	$1.75
10230	**Sam Chance** Benjamin Capps	$1.25
82091	**Tragg's Choice** Clifton Adams	$1.75
82135	**The Trail To Ogallala** Benjamin Capps	$1.25
85903	**The Valdez Horses** Lee Hoffman	$1.75

Available wherever paperbacks are sold or use this coupon.

12H

Sharp Shooting
and
Rugged Adventure
from
America's Favorite
Western Writers

44464	**Kinch** Matt Braun	$1.75
83236	**Twenty Notches** Max Brand	$1.75
56025	**The Nameless Breed** Will C. Brown	$1.50
82403	**Trigger Trio** Ernest Haycox	$1.50
51860	**The Man On The Blood Bay** Kyle Hollingshead $1.50	
04739	**Bandido** Nelson Nye	$1.50
62340	**Omaha Crossing** Ray Hogan	$1.50
81132	**A Time For Vengeance** Giles Lutz	$1.50
87640	**Wear A Fast Gun** John Jakes	$1.50
30675	**Gun Country** Wayne C. Lee	$1.50

Available wherever paperbacks are sold or use this coupon.

🔘 **ace books,** Book Mailing Service,
20 Addison Place, Valley Stream, New York 11580

Please send me titles checked above.

I enclose $............... Add 50¢ handling fee per copy.

Name ....

Address ....

City.................... State............. Zip........